Courtesans — Part I

By
Michael Polowetzky

COURTESANS

Part I

By
MICHAEL POLOWETZKY

ISBN: 978-1-63950-008-6   [Paperback Edition]
      978-1-63950-009-3   [eBook Edition]

Printed and bound in The United States of America.

Writers Apex

Gateway Towards Success

8063 MADISON AVE #1252
Indianapolis, IN 46227
+13176596889
www.writersapex.com

To: DH

Part 1

House of Monfort

Thursday Evening

"NOW, COME! COME, MADEMOISELLE Rolande! Please do, reconsider!"

"Well, I'm not sure…it would be…proper…of me…to…accept, Your…Grace," coyly stammered in reply a fetching teenage redhead in short sleeveless lapis-lazuli-colored dress, neutral-shade pantyhose, and white high heels. Her long, heavy locks were tied back loosely behind head. Crossing her attractive adolescent legs opposite, she sat atop an antique, cherrywood green damask armchair. "I'm not sure if it…would be…proper…of me. Those pieces you're offering must be awesomely…expensive! I'm not sure if…it would be proper…proper of me…accepting them." *Miss Proper* offered a not-so-*proper* wink followed by a not-so-*proper* giggle.

Her aristocratic gift-giver winked back and returned a flirtatious, knowing grin.

"Oh, come, come. Please take them both, Mademoiselle Rolande, dear," again urged Prince Alexander Vladirmovich Markovsky to his fetching quarry.

She was still wavering as to whether to accept the newcomer's fabulous gifts.

"It will make me so pleased, so honored, if you do take them, sweetheart. Consider my gifts as but a trifling visible token of the great inner, personal esteem in which I hold you and your beautiful, ever-so enchanting sister, I mean, *mother*, Madame de Montfort."

In his early fifties, remarkably handsome and he keenly aware, possessing an impressive baritone voice with superb social charm, Markovsky was long accustomed to getting his own way with vulnerable young females, perhaps too often for both *his* and the ingénue's own good. The prince's refined, poised, athletic six-foot-five-inch physique was only appropriate for an individual with so grand a name and historic family lineage.

On this particular Thursday evening in the *Baroque* townhouse at No. 3 Rue Artemis, the wealthy nobleman's imposing frame was clothed in a no less fittingly exorbitant-priced, tailor-made, light-gray three-piece suit. The grandee's tone of speech, his choice of words, and physical comportment were each just as inimitably refined. It all came as effortless as breathing or riding a bicycle, he claimed. Like all male members of this enclosed, privileged, self-perpetuating social circle, the prince was a *gentleman*. His was a personal behavior, a mode of thinking, philosophical worldview impossible for any parvenu, nouveau riche American riffraff to even conceive acquiring. Being a *gentleman* couldn't be learned; it flowed in the blood.

If he was quite fond of telling attractive, impressionable young ladies about his "dark, brooding Russian soul's painful yearning to be once more suckled at the beloved Motherland's holy bosom" and of his "desperate wish to contemplate the true meaning of mankind's tormented epic, troubled saga, while meditating upon the blessed waters of the mighty Volga and heroic, immortal Don," this snappy-clad seducer had in fact never traveled closer to those celebrated lands and rivers than Warsaw. As in the case of most descendents of Tsarist émigrés long settled abroad, the prince was Russian in name alone.

Although the Markovsky family lost vast financial holdings and great rural estates to the Bolsheviks in October 1917, the clan's present leader succeeded in recovering both forms of wealth many times over while living in France. This more recent fortune he obtained through real estate price manipulation, personal banking, insider trading of software and pharmaceutical stocks, cameo television appearances, as well as acquiring intimate ties to venal elected officials and poorly paid, overworked career civil servants open to persuasion. If his *White Russian* ancestors just managed eking by in a Montmartre garret through shining shoes, telling fortunes at fairs, playing the accordion with trained monkey on grubby street corner, their tycoon grandson lived in a sixteenth-century arrondissement palace in the fashionable suburbs.

As chairman of France's largest private investment firm, *Crédit l'Est*, with major figures from all established political blocs securely in his own financial debt, handsome, debonair Prince *Alex* (as he was known in celebrity circles) found his rise to public prominence swift. Rumors were rampant President Thomas Belanger was about to appoint the nobleman as minister of finance.

Last spring, France witnessed not extensive social unrest but near revolution. It united millions of university and secondary school students, academics and middle-class intellectuals, charitable organizations, left-of-center political activists, labor union rank and file, and journalists. The protest movement winning too the loyalty of both housewives and feminists, secularists, and devout believers. The scale and vehemence of the recent nationwide protest movement was reminiscent of May 1968, or as estimated by many historians, was similar to even earlier, far more cataclysmic moments in French history.

Caught, like all chieftains of the long-entrenched conservative government, completely off guard, suave up-and-coming Prince Markovsky was delivered a dreadful, existential fright, one more alarming than he would ever choose to reveal. Then, just as the revolution's triumph was at hand, its spiritual inspiration, four-foot-ten-inch teenage Middle Eastern refugee artist Pascale Kedari, increasingly called by her more devout and romantic followers *Little Marie*, was assassinated by a terrorist.

Without miniature *Little Marie*'s idealistic, unifying presence, the revolution she inspired and her thought-provoking frescoes that gave such charismatic voice, seemed to sputter out almost as speedily as it once engulfed all French society. The violent backlash at the next parliamentary election, restoring the right to power, appeared to confirm this sad verdict. If great cathedrals, historic plazas, famous boulevards, and noted theaters throughout the country were still haunted by the magical refugee girl's artistic masterpieces, *Little Marie* and the uprising she only months earlier ignited, appeared today, save for a tiny band of faithful original disciples, as distant in time as Giotto and the Middle Ages.

"Come, come, Mademoiselle Rolande, please do reconsider," the prince encouraged. "I'll be so honored for you to accept my gifts. If you're worried about the price, don't let your little head be troubled for an instant. The diamonds come from my own collection. As for the sable coat, that clotheshorse Princess Markovskaya will never know it's even gone."

"But I don't know...if it would be...*proper*," coyly stammered the young redhead. "I feel—"

"My child's simply overwhelmed! Taken aback at such immense generosity, Your Grace!" swiftly cut in Madame de Montfort, seated just beside.

With her high forehead and cheekbones; cherry-blond hair falling to bare shoulders; fragrant, smooth, firm, unblemished rosy skin; strong chin; good teeth; straight nose; elegant neck; fetching, alluring green eyes and red-painted smile; fine bust and splendid feminine body in long strapless white opera gown, the chatelaine looked more like her daughter's near look-alike big sister than parent.

"My *Missy* simply needs more time to take it all in!" pledged her elegant mother. "My child's obviously at a loss for the right words to adequately express her deep, deep, deep appreciation."

"Is the *little dear* ill, Celine?" queried the prince, anxious. "I certainly didn't mean upsetting the *sweet thing*. I merely wished demonstrating my deep admiration for her through these gifts."

"No, no, Your Grace. She's not ill," assured Madame de Montfort. "As I said, *Missy* is simply stunned at this degree of generosity! She's unable to find adequate words just yet...perhaps if you were to return on Sunday? I guarantee by Sunday, the child will be able to better express her thanks."

"Sunday you said, Celine?"

"Yes, on Sunday about seven in the evening, Your Grace."

"I could naturally leave the presents here now, but I much prefer offering them in the old-fashion, traditional manner. I'm after all an old-fashion, traditional gentleman."

"Ah!" sighed Madame de Montfort, redoing her lipstick and mascara. "If only today's eat-or-be-eaten, Americanized, rat-race, materialistic, pagan world possessed more old-fashion, traditional gentlemen like Your Grace! How so much better we weak, *scatterbrained* women could be protected, be kept in hand, our fragile little needs best seen to!"

"So until Sunday at seven in the evening, say, my little ladies?"

"So until Sunday at seven in the evening say, *your* little ladies."

Picking up his gloves, scarf, and long heavy-tailored overcoat, Prince Markovsky turned to leave.

"Bonsoir!" called the young redhead after her new distinguished chum, voice both meek and coquettish. "So it's bonsoir until Sunday evening at seven, my noble, famous champion!"

"So it's bonsoir until Sunday evening at seven to you too, my *sweet thing*," replied Prince Markovsky with roguish smile and teasing gesture of right hand.

Redhead threw him a kiss.

Markovsky threw a kiss to redhead.

The pair winked at one another confidingly.

Each waved back in same flirtatious manner.

Guest departed.

Mother and daughter were once more alone.

"Bravo! Bravo! Mama says you were positively superb, *Missy!*" exclaimed Mme. de Montfort. She was seated ladylike atop a cherrywood red damask armchair in her townhouse's first floor *Louis XV*-styled parlor. Nearby *French windows* provide immediate access to an enclosed well-tended *Continental* garden, where stood tall oriental vases containing glorious fragrant bouquets of rambling roses, hydrangeas, hollyhocks, crocus, irises, orchids, anemones, violets, carnations, and delphiniums.

"You're certainly Mama's child!" extolled Marie-Therese-Celine de Montfort, known by her intimates simply as *Celine*. "You're certainly Mama's creation! As Mama did first to your sister Ferdinande and so again to you, she passed on all her best genes! All her best *DNA*! She secured each of her lovely girls permanently at the head of the social food chain! Permanently at the top of their generation's cultural pecking order!" She concluded, "No blood test will ever be required to demonstrate to whose womb you and Ferdinande belong!"

"Thank you so much, Mama," answered Rolande modestly, crossing her legs opposite, hem of short lapis-lazuli-colored dress receding. "I'm so glad you think I did a good job. I know there's nothing that excites characters with trousers more than ladies playing *hard to get.*"

"So correct you are, love!" observed Celine approvingly. "There's nothing which excites those characters with trousers more than ladies playing *hard to get.*"

She applied a soft, maternal shielding kiss to her child's unblemished forehead and stroked affectionately her daughter's long red hair.

"Still, let Mama give you one ever so slight piece of advice. Next Sunday, when Prince Markovsky again offers you that splendid necklace and fabulous coat, feel absolutely no inhibition. Accept them both immediately."

Celine paused…giggled, sly.

"Remember, cherie, if you don't accept these gifts soon, who knows what the future may have in store? Monday, our generous benefactor might be hit by a bus!"

"Indeed, Mama. Carpe diem, *seize the moment.*"

"Besides, my darling," explained Celine, "it's only good, ladylike manners to accept tokens of appreciation from a prince! Last month, I understood it was only good ladylike manners for me to say yes when the prince asked if I would accept his Picasso!"

"Yes, Mama."

"However, other than that teeny, tiny, teensy, ever-so-easily-fixed point, *Missy,* you're performance this evening was beauty. Splendor itself! I'm so proud of my gifted little girl. I know that one day my dear is going to win herself a prince!"

"I'll really one day win myself a prince, Mama?"

"So indeed you will, my superb *Missy!* You'll win yourself a prince, a *prince charming.*"

"Oh, Mama!" replied Rolande, turning away, demure, crossing her lovely legs opposite, tossing back her waist-length fiery red hair with a single motion of sculpted neck. "But remember too, Mama, I've the most awesome teacher there is! A teacher more awesome than awesome can awesomely ever awesomely be! 'We stand on the shoulders of giants!' says Sir Isaac Newton. But I stand on the shoulders of a *giantess*! Don't forget, people say it's not only nature that counts, it's also nurture."

"Bless you, my sweetest, most tender offspring!"

"Can I now have permission to go and watch television, Mama?"

"If you promise not turning it up too loud."

"I promise."

"And promise Mama that you'll go to sleep on time?"

"Yes, Mama, I promise to go to sleep on time."

"And remember to say all your prayers to the Virgin?"

"Yes, Mama, I promise to say all my prayers to the Virgin."

"Promise to ask her intercession for the poor people in the terrible flood?"

"Yes, Mama, I promise to ask the Virgin to intercede for the poor people in the terrible flood."

"Well then, Mama gives permission for her *Missy* to watch television. Run along…wait! But first don't forget to give your mama a big kiss."

"I won't forget to give my mama a big kiss!"

Parent and child embraced fondly.

"Ah, thanks, *Missy!* You make a proud mother's heart feel so happy!"

"I love you, Mama!"

"I love you too, *Missy*! Now give your mama one more kiss and run along."

I

Montfort wasn't the name of Rolande's father, of course. This particular individual's real identity and current whereabouts his daughter never learned.

"If that mysterious gentleman wishes remaining a stranger," concluded Rolande at age only four, "I won't waste my valuable time seeking the rascal out!" She soon added, "Besides, with a Mama as *awesome* as mine, a father would only get in the way!"

Countess Marie-Therese-Celine de Montfort is indeed an *awesome* personality, her life story far from the humdrum or uneventful. Those privileged encountering this august dame might, with perfect logic, assume she recently exited a John Singer Sargent portrait, an Edith Wharton novel, or just emerged from a Gordon Park's fashion shot in *Vogue*.

The countess regally maintains two large historic *Baroque* Parisian townhouses with staffs of devoted liveried servants as well as a third no-less-magnificent eighteenth-century residence in Bordeaux. In addition, she boasts grand country villas with extensive adjoining property in Brittany, Normandy, the French Alps, and the Riviera. She drives only a *Ferrari* or *Jaguar* and flies her own *Huey* attack helicopter. She owns not a stitch of clothing except strapless opera gowns; stylish, short low-necked dresses; exotic lingerie; Vicuna coats; and the most expensive and fashionable skirts, blouses, hosiery, chapeaus, gloves, scarves, shawls, and heels. All this, the countess either easily purchases, ably administers, or alluringly wears, though she received not a day of formal education or possessing any visible source of income.

Far from a hedonist dedicated merely to material gain and personal enjoyment however, Celine is also celebrated as "the female Horowitz," and as the "Rubinstein-in-a-skirt." She is uniformly acknowledged as the finest concert pianist in Europe. "No one has truly heard the piano works of Bach, Mozart, Beethoven, Chopin, Brahms, Tchaikovsky, Schumann, Mendelssohn, Prokofiev, or Grieg," esteemed music critics unanimously concur, "until they are played with the benefit of this unique artist's delicate, painted fingers." Dedicating all the receipts to charity, this lady is a dedicated, highly successful, and much sought-after fundraiser and spokesperson for worthy social and religious causes.

And what of Madame's views on public affairs? If always supporting the mainline conservatives on polling day, the countess belongs to no specific party. She much prefers steering far from "that dreary, back-stabbing, *men's issue*."

"Politics," insists Celine emphatically, "is much too convoluted, tangled, byzantine for ladies to ever possibly understand." Politics "is far too cold-blooded, rough-and-tumble for ladies with our fragile sensibilities, delicate physical constitutions to long endure."

"Government," she often stresses, "is best left to people who wear trousers. Can you imagine national leadership, statecraft, decision-making, or matters of life-and-death being the responsibility of *witless women*? Blessed Virgin! No, thank you! Nor did God ever intend it to be so! Remember, what's happened to us all after Eve tasted the forbidden fruit!"

One consequence of Celine's professed judgment of the *weaker sex* is that her principal *Baroque* townhouse in Paris soon acquired, and thereafter easily retained, powerful and influential gentlemen belonging to all sides of the political and business spectrum. No. 3 Rue Artemis is a favorite address for both communists and monarchists. It has long been a haven for cabinet officers in both right-of-center governments and socialist ones. Visits to No. 3 Rue Artemis are savored as much by robber barons and captains of industry as by union leaders and radical social reformers. This lovely residence is cherished by revolutionaries no less than by champions of the status quo.

By carefully avoiding outward controversy, apolitical Celine is better informed about top-secret intelligence, about critical domestic and international economic developments, military operations, and matters of foreign policy than nearly every government official and elected legislator. She is already well-versed on these valuable revelations long before they ever reach the ears of top financiers, securities traders, real estate speculators, the press, and, certainly, the general public. Her patrons become so dependent upon Celine to relieve them of the heavy emotional and physical strain come with exercising authority that they soon invite her into their own personal confidence. She, in a short time, becomes for each political leader, diplomat, general, stockjobber, or business CEO his closest, most trusted intimate.

First just a deferential, sympathetic listener, Celine skillfully graduates to a provider of superb unrecognized advice, masterful uncredited guidance.

"Fantastic, Baron!"

"Marvelous, Monsignor!"

"Unprecedented, Mr. President!"

"You're such a genius, Monsieur!" dutifully chirps the lady as yet another distinguished client eagerly divulges further government top secrets, additional stock exchange insider-trading tips. "I'm only a scatterbrained female. Still, I just can't resist asking if my own heroic Napoleon, my own noble Tristan, might possibly next consider trying *such and such* and then perhaps doing *this and that*? Maybe afterward, he should then *go here, not there*. But don't mind me, master. You're the brainy one. You're the one who must make the decision. It's not a woman's place to meddle in these serious matters!"

Celine is keenly aware "how brittle is the male ego." She is sure so that each time one of her seeming vapid, *dumb blond* suggestions bears fruit in her patron's next achievement, He never once doubts this exceptional deed, historic reform, was entirely his own brilliant masculine idea.

"A wise, farsighted, born leader of men like you, master," the grand courtesan assures her political kingmaker or business tycoon, "never requires my poor flibbertigibbet's counsel."

It is an institution at No. 3 Rue Artemis, which Celine is not foundress but mere current caretaker. Like her almost equally noteworthy sisters Philippine Luria, operating the branch of the family business located in Berlin, and Léonie Golitsyn, directing their station in London, Celine is meticulous in training her own fetching daughters to steadfastly continue the clan's five-hundred-and-fifty-year-old tradition. Like her siblings, Celine is quite confident the House of Montfort will be perpetuated in the same renowned style and unique spirit for generations to come.

II

It wasn't inaccurate to say Rolande inherited all of Mama's "best genes and best *DNA*." Able to sign her name at age three, fully literate in her native French at four, she become fluent in the first of eventually seven foreign languages by six. This daughter with the fiery locks never asked her Mama *what* but rather *why.* Followed in short order by *show me why* and *are you sure that's why* and finally *why not this other way I thought of instead*? Rolande never cared for dolls or playing house, she far preferred toy soldiers, electrical trains, chemistry sets, model airplanes, and pondering historical maps.

Rolande never wet the bed, fiddled with her food, left a mess, or believed in Santa Claus. Once, she needed climbing into Mama's bed after a nightmare in which Cardinal Richelieu wanted to lock the child in the Bastille. Unlike the average youngster taken to the pediatrician for shots, rather than cry, attempt to resist, this particular one instead bravely rolled back her sleeve and offered the doctor her little arm. Once, the girl even inquired if she needed a shot against the *Black Death*. When at games with other kids, she refused to "let the boy win."

Each weekend morning, Rolande rose faithfully at 6:00 a.m. not to watch cartoons but to see ministry of agriculture documentaries on modern farming. "It might not seem so at the start, Mama," she once explained over breakfast, "but fertilizer is a fascinating subject! And so is industrial-scale milk production!"

This singular child could recite the names of all the crowned-rulers of France and their consorts back to Clovis—in reverse! She as well can name all the chemical components in the recipes needed for producing the colors of stained glass found in *Gothic* cathedrals. She read Dante and Petrarca in the original Italian. On the table beside her bed, she kept a framed photograph not of a *pop*star or sports hero but of the philosopher and political activist Simone Weil.

"I so love my Simone Weil with her big glasses, Mama," once confided Rolande as Celine entered her daughter's bedroom to provide a mother's good-night kiss. "Simone's big glasses make her look so approachable, so accessible, so vulnerable, so much of another real little girl! Those big glasses of hers help us remember there was a time when my Simone actually walked this earth! When she took flesh! Remind us there was a time when my Simone actually walked and lived among us! When my Simone suffered for us all! Took the punishment for our own misdeeds! She was both a genius, far up there above us all, and a genius far up there above us all who would also want to sit down and talk to us! My Simone would want to know our own opinion! She'd ask if we needed her help, ask if she could join us, encourage us!"

Rolande said, "My Simone was awesome! She was positively awesome! Don't you agree, Mama? Agree too that my Simone was *awesome*! Some people think she is plain. Foolishness! She might not have been... beautiful... in the humdrum ordinary sense. But I think she has a sweet face. I think my Simone Weil is cute! A genius who is cute! It's hard to think of another. Can you, Mama?"

"Sorry," admitted Mama, applying a warm kiss to daughter's forehead. "Sorry, I can't think of another such person at the moment. Now go to sleep, Missy."

"Mama, do you think other people we know are also interested in Simone?"

"It's difficult to say, my little philosopher. I'm not sure the other people we meet ever travel in such lofty circles."

"Do you think other people we know understand how Simone is so awesome? Because talking about my Simone is so much fun!"

"Go to sleep now, *Missy*. We'll have lots of time to talk about your Simone Weil tomorrow."

"Do you promise?"

"Yes, Mama promises! After all, what would Simone Weil think of Mama if she didn't keep a promise?"

Heretofore, an expert womanizer Prince Markovsky, by entering the sphere of the famous *Montfort Ladies*, was getting himself involved in far more than he bargained.

Following Sunday

"WHAT CAN I SAY, Your Grace?" answered Rolande, Jackie Kennedy-breathless, as Prince Markovsky again offered her a museum-quality diamond necklace and ankle-length sable coat. "What more can I say other than that I'm tremendously honored, awesomely grateful! What more can I say than that I'll be forever indebted. I'll never be able to repay, Your Grace, for such immense freely chosen kindness." Redhead curtseyed deep, sniffled, batted eyes, and smiled humbly.

"Hail to the Virgin!" exclaimed Mama, strapless, her lovely bare shoulders, arms, and back employed for genteel emphasis. "They're both fabulous, Your Grace! Missy looks magnificent! You have such ideal taste! What could weak women do without you?"

"Let me simply say how immensely honored I am to receive them, Your Grace," repeated Rolande, also dipping her pretty head, bending knee, her own fine bare arms, shoulders, and back offering additional sign of vulnerable feminine respect. All gestures she performed in a single, instinctive, unbroken ladylike motion. A beckoning innocent twinkle showed in the teenager's large brown eyes. "I hope I'll be worthy of wearing them."

"I already know you will, dear," assured Prince Markovsky.

Rolande gave him a humble peck on right cheek.

"Isn't the *sweetheart* beautiful, perfect, priceless, Celine?" commented the prince to Mme. de Montfort.

She, once again, was seated next to daughter, just beside.

After first clipping a stunning chain of large white, dark-red, and green diamonds about Rolande's gentle sculpted neck, Markovsky proceeded to wrap a long, thick, white fifty-thousand-dollar sable coat about the body of his newest young dalliance. Careful all the while, he still left exposed the girl's fine, youthful bare shoulders. That done, her benefactor stepped back a few paces to admire his own creation. "Splendid! You do indeed look splendid, *Missy!*"

"Splendid!" endorsed Mama. "And all thanks to Your Grace!"

"The diamonds are from India during the *Mogul Period*," explained the dapper gent, ever fond of recounting the exploits of his colorful forbears. "The diamond necklace is from roughly 1690, during the reign of Aurangzeb. It was acquired by one of my ancestors, the original Prince Alexander Markovsky. He and Peter the Great were the best of personal chums. Besides military campaigns and political maneuverings, the duo much enjoyed drinking and going to the whorehouse together," he mused. "The original *Prince Alexander Markovsky* was also once dispatched by the tsar to explore India."

"Fascinating, Your Grace!" bubbled Mama.

"Well," confessed the dapper gent mischievously, "*explore* was just the diplomatic term used. The original Alexander Markovsky, you can find him in all history books of Russia, came across these magnificent stones during one of his early travels. To tell you the truth, he was supposed to deliver all the stones he discovered to the tsar. But seeing as how Peter the Great already possessed far more diamonds than he could ever possibly count and also wasn't paying my ancestor anything to go on this expedition, the original Prince Alexander decided it was only fair he be...compensated...in kind."

His descendant further explained this evening in Paris, "The sable coat comes from Russia before October 1917. My grandfather, Prince Nikita, once served as foreign minister as well as, for a time, minister of the secret police and governor general of Siberia. As result, he was provided unique access to the best furs. He was provided unique access to the best furs at the price he personally thought most reasonable." Markovsky paused, reflective. "How does that old Russian folksong I taught you go, Celine, dear? The one with the words from which Turgenev used to entitle a famous novella."

"*Days so happy/years so gay/are like spring torrents/now passed away.*"

"Yes, Celine, that's right exactly! So glad you reminded me. You've got such a good memory for a woman! I swear, honey, you're almost as smart as a man!"

"Ooh! Ooh! Did you hear that, *Missy*?" squealed Madame de Montfort. "Ooh! Ooh! Did you hear that, *Missy*? His Grace says your mama is almost as smart as a man!"

"But don't wear that pretty little blond head of yours out, Celine, honey," advised the prince. "I don't want that charming little brain of yours overtaxed. Too much thinking isn't good for a woman! Too much thinking isn't good for her frail constitution and gentle heart."

"I promise not to wear out my little brain with too much thinking, Your Grace. I know too much thinking makes a woman, even one like me, ill."

"Excellent, excellent. That's my fine, obedient girl."

The prince pecked Mama protectively on her cheeks and fondly caressed her long, thick cherry-blond hair.

"All the same!" Celine giggled, looking away demurely. "To be told I'm almost as smart as man! What an honor! To be told I'm almost as smart as a man!"

The lady's mastery of Rachmaninov's Third Piano Concerto in D Minor was equaled only by her ability to *play dumb*.

"Your Grace comes from such a distinguished family!" Celine declared. "Meeting you is the same as meeting history! You're so tall, handsome...strong too! Say, aren't you even actually related to Peter the Great?"

"Yes, but only distantly!"

"Still all the same! Say, I hear that Peter the Great was seven feet tall."

"Actually, he was only six foot eight. But in a time when the average height for European males was just five foot two...you've seen clothing in museums?"

"Yes."

"Six foot eight must've appeared more like eight feet today."

"Every single part of a Russian man's body is so big!"

"It's a big country, Celine."

"Don't you love them, *sweet thing?*" Prince Markovsky questioned Rolande. "The marvelous stones and grand sable coat are both fitting for a tsarina! An empress! What could any female possibly desire more in her wildest dreams?"

"The marvelous stones and grand sable coat are fitting for a tsarina, Your Grace," repeated Rolande meekly, her loyal eyes linking with those of her wealthy, titled benefactor. "The diamonds and sable coat you gave me are fitting for an empress! What could any female possibly desire more in her wildest dreams?" She curtseyed deep, her fiery red hair falling over her pretty blushing face.

"Now don't fear I've ignored you, Celine, my pet!" Prince Markovsky assured Mama. "No need you cry or be jealous. Don't be upset, my faithful darling. I've remembered my other *sweet thing* too!"

Taking a small pink box from his tailored jacket's right breast pocket, the amorous grandee removed a fabulous green diamond set on a pure gold band. He placed it on Madame de Montfort's left ring finger.

"This stone too my ancestor discovered on his travels to Mogul India in the 1690s. Remember, it was originally meant for the hand of Peter the Great—the most famous, most important figure in all of Russian history! Instead, it is henceforth on your own far much lovelier hand! I can't possibly think of another lady in all of God's creation more worthy of having Peter the Great's diamond on her pretty, delicate, little hand than you, my dainty Celine!"

"Ooh! Ooh! It's tremendous, Your Grace! Ooh! Ooh!" Mama chirped. "Ooh! Ooh! It's positively tremendous, Your Grace!"

She extended her left arm with the incomparable stone now on ring finger to observe it from several angles. The light from crystal chandelier above made the diamond twinkle.

"Ooh! Ooh! It's tremendous, Your Grace! Ooh! Ooh! I promise never to remove it from my finger! Even if doing so would save me from the guillotine! Please, please trust me, Your Grace. I really, really, really

24

mean it! Ooh! Ooh! You certainly know how to make females happy! Ooh! Ooh!" Mama loyally kissed Prince Markovsky's right cheek.

He pawed her bare shoulders, proprietary.

"Shouldn't we go now, Your Grace?" suggested Mama, after first providing her guest time to give his hostess a good *feel.*

At last wriggling out of the prince's amorous grip, mother yanked daughter into own previous position. Never picky, Markovsky's large hands now groped Rolande's bare shoulders, arms, and back, proprietary.

"We don't want to be stalled by traffic do we, Your Grace?" hinted Mama softly. "Especially, since this is opening night. It's *Boris Godunov*, your favorite opera. The one you are so concerned that I follow and appreciate."

"Yes, indeed, Celine," the prince acknowledged, his groping paws still otherwise engaged. "Yes, this evening is opening night you know. Tonight is my favorite opera, *Boris Godunov.* It's the work I'm so concerned my two *little ladies* follow and appreciate."

Markovsky began singing a famous aria off-key.

"Especially," urged Mama, "since this is *Missy's* very first time! Going to the opera is a totally new experience for her. Although the child's been able to pick up seven foreign languages, she's never learned Russian. Maybe it's the different alphabet, I don't know. So this evening, *Missy* will be entirely dependent on you to understand what the singers are saying. She'll be ever so indebted for your kind, fatherly assistance and for the kind, fatherly assistance of such a cultivated nobleman! Won't you be, *Missy*?"

"Indeed, Mama! Indeed!" answered Rolande, also *playing dumb*. First, clutching the handsome gentleman's left arm, she then softly rubbed her right cheek against her wealthy male champion's left shoulder. "I'm absolutely confident the great Prince Alexander Vladimirovich Markovsky will take good care of me, Mama. He'll look after me properly, Mama. He'll explain to me everything he thinks is proper I need to know. Maybe he can even teach me to speak Russian."

"Rolande is fluent in seven foreign languages, you say, Celine?" asked Markovsky, thoughtful.

"So *Missy* is, Your Grace. She's totally fluent in seven foreign languages!"

"That's most commendable! You've raised her well. Fluency in seven foreign languages can make a woman most useful to a man."

Traffic was heard outside, voices too.

"Don't you think it's time we leave!" pressed Mama, again diplomatic.

"So correct you are, Celine. It's also opening night," reiterated Markovsky, much pleased with himself, convinced he was actually the one taking the initiative. "It's time we three should leave. We must not get stalled by traffic. In a half hour or so, that section of the city becomes so terribly congested. Besides, it's opening night. My limousine should be already outside. I enjoy nothing better than bringing pleasure to lovely, gracious ladies, above all when those ladies are named Madame and Mademoiselle de Montfort!"

"What a gentleman you are!" declared Mama, taking the prince's other arm. "What a gentleman you are, Your Grace!"

The grandee departed the *Louis XV-style* salon, a pretty female on each his arm.

"So this is indeed your first live experience of the opera, dear?" the prince queried Rolande as the fashionable threesome descended the *Baroque* townhouse's wrought-iron front steps, exited the tall gate, then climbed into a sleek, shiny, feline black stretch limousine. Not too surreptitiously, the prince also evaluated the teenager's nice, young, healthily expanding bust. As a noted connoisseur of young, healthily expanding busts, the favorable judgment Markovsky drew of this latest example should be well respected.

"Yes, Your Grace!" said Rolande. "It's my very first opera."

The weather this evening was Indian summer. The temperature in Paris, gently cool. A soft, relaxing breeze stroked the clear air.

"Well then, depend on me, dear," pledged the titled plutocrat. "As your Mama knows, I'm quite an expert on opera. I've likely talked off Celine's ear on the subject long ago! My grandfather, you must understand, actually knew Chaliapin and Caruso! He listened to Chaliapin sing *Boris Godunov* back in Russia before the 1917 Revolution!"

"Awesome!" was Rolande's prompt reply, Jackie Kennedy—breathless.

"My grandfather also attended the famous first performance in which Caruso sang *La Juive*. Toscanini conducted the orchestra!"

"Awesome!"

"My father knew the great Geraldine Farrar. He was even present when she first sang *Madame Butterfly*."

"That's *really* awesome, Your Grace!" extolled Rolande. "Auntie Philippine knows I enjoy hearing opera. Auntie Philippine gave me all these antique recordings of Geraldine Farrar and Lily Pons. Unfortunately, they're on thick *72 LPs*, and it's impossible at the moment for me to play them."

"My father also personally knew the incomparable Lily Pons! He listened to her great opening performance at La Scala of *Lucia di Lammermoor*."

"Awesome! That's positively ever so, so *really* awesome!"

"I'm a good friend of Bryn Terfel," next boasted Prince Markovsky, giving Rolande another *feel*. "I've watched and heard Bryn Terfel in his first appearance in *Don Giovanni*. During that season, he also alternated with Lukasz Golinski in the two major roles, one night taking the part of the Don and then on the other singing the role of Leporello."

"They're both baritone roles after all, Your Grace!" interjected Rolande. "Each has an almost corresponding role. It reminds me in a way of Othello and Iago in Shakespeare! Remember Verdi made an opera out of the play!"

"Are you absolutely sure you've never been to the opera before, dear?" asked Prince Markovsky, wide smile on his aristocratic lips, twinkle in lordly brown eyes.

"No, it's true, Your Grace!" insisted Rolande. "Up until now I only know opera from television or listening to recordings. Not those 72s, of course. Although it would be nice to one day listen to them. Auntie Philippine is so enthusiastic about Geraldine Farrar."

"Well! This is the start of a brilliant season, dear," guaranteed Prince Markovsky. "No better time for you to graduate from watching opera simply on television or hearing it on recordings and possessing Auntie Philippine's old records you can't play. This is no better time for you to see opera with your own eyes. Who knows! The day may come, sooner than you expect, when you're as devoted to it as I am! This season should be most impressive. Besides *Boris Godunov,* there will be *Norma, Don Carlos, Otello, Prince Igor, Aida, Rigoletto, Manon Lescaut, Tristan und Isolde, Il Trovatore, Flying Dutchman, La Traviata, Elektra, La Boheme, Carmen.*"

"*Carmen!*" answered Rolande, excited, eager to further reveal her own knowledge of the subject. "I learned that the composer, Georges Bizet, was the son-in-law of Jacques Halévy, who composed *La Juive*! And Bizet's wife, Genevieve—Halévy's daughter—was also a great chum of Marcel Proust."

"Those Yids certainly stick together!"

"Genevieve Bizet often appears in Proust's writing under another name!" continued the erudite youngster. "Proust was once the opera critic for *Figaro*! Proust portrays all three of them—Georges Bizet, Genevieve Bizet, and her father Jacques Halévy in *A la Recherche du Temps Perdu*!"

"You've definitely caught the opera bug, dear!" exclaimed the prince with delight. "I already can tell you'll soon be as passionate on the subject as me!"

"Well, if I have caught the bug," answered Rolande humbly, "I know I caught the bug from Your Grace!"

Markovsky pawed the girl's bare shoulders, proprietary. He pecked the teenager's unblemished forehead as if entitled. "You're my *sweet thing*!"

"I hope I'll be a good one, Your Grace."

The nobleman hummed a famous aria, off-key.

Rolande hummed the same heroic song, in tune.

Her illustrious companion pawed her again.

"This is really exciting, Mama!" cried daughter. "It's so wonderful of Prince Markovsky to take me to the opera! It's so wonderful Prince Markovsky can take me to the opera and be my special guide and instructor!"

"If you enjoy tonight as much as it appears you will," offered the prince, "can I be so bold as to escort you to the opera again? I told you the next production going to be Bellini's *Norma*. That's another one of my favorites. *Norma* is another opera which I hope will soon be one of your own favorites, my dear."

"I'll be delighted, Your Grace!"

"Naturally, being the *old-fashion*, traditional, formal gentleman I am," advised Prince Markovsky, "I'll be expecting your mama to come as our chaperone."

"No, no!" Celine intervened. "There's no need for Mama coming too, Your Grace. My own concert performance schedule is busy for the next several months. I must go back to my piano and get another hour of practice before retiring to bed early. I'm confident *Missy* will be safe in your princely hands from now on."

Excellent Prospects

Boris Godunov
Norma
Don Carlos
Otello
Prince Igor
Aida
Rigoletto
Manon Lescaut
Tristan und Isolde
Il Trovatore
Flying Dutchman
La Traviata
Elektra
La Boheme

Carmen

FIRST, WEEKS, THEN MONTHS elapsed. Every masterpiece was returned to the stage and orchestra pit in the same unforgettable, superb fashion. No one privileged attending them was rash enough to try ranking the productions in order of quality. Each rendering of the famous composers' work was magnificent. Singers, audiences, members of the orchestra, music scholars, even newspaper critics ever eager to find fault, unanimously agreed that many decades were passed since Paris last presented such a brilliant and memorable opera season. Few attending these celebrated performances, however, were as enthusiastic about the experience as Mademoiselle de Montfort.

Missy was driven to the exclusive opening night of all twelve reproductions in Prince Markovsky's sleek shiny, feline black stretch limousine. Each time the land battleship carrying the lucky girl arrived, *paparazzi* catering to low-brow, cutthroat competition, mass-distribution British, German, Italian and Spanish right-wing tabloids madly snapped their complicated Japanese gadgets as France's newest celebrity made her pretty, genteel appearance. *Missy*'s muscular, six-foot-six, liveried Turkish chauffeur, fifty hollow-nose bullet-clip semiautomatic at belt, always first opened the passenger door to provide the teenager his own chivalric assistance. She then stylishly emerged in what Mama taught was the only manner appropriate for ladies to exit vehicles. By now instinctively offering the swarming photographers a beaming, innocent smile on her painted lips, clutching Prince Markovsky's right arm, *Missy* was dressed on each succeeding glamorous occasion in yet another beautiful strapless gown her aristocratic billionaire, politically ambitious male companion decided purchasing for his newest toy.

Even before entering the ornate Second-Empire-style hall to watch the performance from Prince Markovsky's private box, his young friend felt mysteriously transported back to *La Belle Époque.* She received the marvelous sensation of returning to that towering era of French artistic, cultural, intellectual, and spiritual achievement during the roughly three and a half decades before the outbreak of the Great War. If outside, a self-consumed humanity trudged along in the humdrum, lackluster, rat-race current age within the Garnier l'Opéra, *Missy* was permitted becoming a close chum, an eager personal friend of Proust, Colette, Zola, Verlaine, Paul Claudel, Debussy, Frank, Saint-Saens, Ravel, Monet, Renoir, Cezanne, Gaugin, Matisse, Chagall, Toulouse-Lautrec, Braque, Marie and Pierre Curie, Henri Poincaré; Bergson, Rodin, Camille Claudel, *The Divine Sarah* (Bernhardt), St. Therese of Lisieux.

Following each successive opera performance and bath in tabloid photographer's flashbulb's glare came for the lucky girl another drive in Markovsky's sleek, shiny, feline black stretch limousine. The journey carrying her to the prince's grand *Baroque* palace located within a sprawling, enclosed, wooded estate situated in the exclusive Parisian suburb of Neuilly. Once arrived, the couple first discussed the recent performance while resting upon overstuffed, cherrywood damask *Queen Anne* armchairs. Finally, the pair withdrew until morning inside an elegant, sumptuous, Watteau fresco-ceiling private room with large, oak, canopied four-poster bed.

I

"So I really am *that terrific?*" pleaded an exhausted male partner in gasping, wheezing voice, his middle-aged body drenched in sweat, his lungs throbbing, heart racing. "So I really, truly am *that terrific?*"

"Ooh, yes, yes, Your Grace," assured *Missy*, relaxed and cheery. "Yes, you really are *that terrific!* You're everything any woman can ever possibly want! Now do it to me again, Your Grace! Do it to me again!"

"Can we first please rest for a few minutes, sweetheart?" implored the weary king-making plutocrat. He panted, rolling over dead tired to the other side of wide mattress. "I think that in showing you how I'm *that terrific*, I've also given myself a wretched backache, twisted my left leg."

II

"As long as I keep telling the *little thing* just what she wants to hear," later boasted Markovsky to his image in bathroom mirror, shaving. "As long as I cater to the creature's natural feminine vanity, she'll be no difficulty bending to my own will."

The prince added, washing the razor in the sink, "True, she possesses more brains than is appropriate for a woman. However, she knows never to challenge her master. That the girl also enjoys opera provides me a chance to further display my own wide expertise."

III

During one overnight visit to his suburban estate, the prince employed a complicated Japanese gadget to transpose Auntie Philippine's classic recordings from old, now unplayable *72 LPs* on to modern *CDs*, thus enabling Rolande to at last hear the beautiful voice of Geraldine Farrar in Puccini's *Madame Butterfly*. On another sojourn at Neuilly, the nobleman transposed modern recordings of Lily Pons staring in Donizetti's *Lucia di Lammermoor.*

"Thank you ever so much for the gift, Your Grace!" pledged the novice courtesan. "I'm eternally indebted, Your Grace!"

"Don't mention it," answered the moneyed schemer, quite proud of himself. "There's nothing I enjoy more than seeing my little darling smile."

Summons on the Embankment

"IT'S IMPORTANT I SEE you again very soon, *sweet thing,"* explained Prince Alexander Vladirmovich Markovsky in the early morning hours after *Carmen* brought this year's Paris opera season to a brilliant conclusion.

He first assisted *Missy* down the sweeping white marble front staircase of his family's rambling seventeenth-century mansard-roof palace. Next, he escorted her across the gravel pathway leading to awaiting black stretch limousine. Then he helped the girl into the second-row passenger seat before, at last, closing the huge vehicle's door behind her, proprietary.

Finally, Markovsky instructed his liveried Turkish chauffeur to deliver his charge still not old enough to vote back into the custody of her mama located in more central Paris.

"Being with you is so rewarding, *sweet thing."*

"I'm so deeply touched, Your Grace," replied *Missy*, forcing a blush as she spoke out from behind the car's open bulletproof window. "You must indeed come again for me soon, Your Grace!"

"What about next weekend? I've got an event you might enjoy attending with me. So much do I love showing you off, making others jealous of my recent precious discovery! So next weekend then?"

"Oh, yes certainly! I'll be delighted to be taken, Your Grace."

"Just as I'd hoped, *sweet thing.* You'll hear from me in a few days. Give my regards to Celine. I certainly can tell you're her daughter!"

"Thank you, Your Grace."

Prince Markovsky took Rolande's hands firmly in his larger own, kissing them. At last releasing them, he stepped back and ordered the spacious limousine to set off.

I

Upon exiting the high red-brick enclosing wall of his employer's wooded estate, the chauffeur soon made a left.

Next, a right.

Then another.

A left.

A second left.

Finally, the driver piloted the massive vehicle straight ahead.

The stretch limousine freely navigated the wide avenues and parks, easily traversed the graceful bridges on its journey back to central Paris. Scant traffic at this early hour made the trip both swift and quiet. With nothing to distract her attention or interrupt her musings, the lovely passenger reviewed her actions over the months since she first traveled in this prestigious land battleship.

"Mama will be ever so proud of me!" commented her daughter, appraising her rookie performance as a *Montfort Lady*. "I've done just as Mama taught me!"

And so Celine's attentive offspring certainly did.

In the course of the just concluded Paris opera season, Rolande eagerly accepted a pirate's treasure of *Mogul Period* diamond tiaras, necklaces, and hairpins; *Safavid Dynasty* Persian rubies to decorate her fingers and earlobe; *Ancien Regime* brooches and cameos for her bust; long strings of Japanese natural pearls; vicuna coats and exquisite silk strapless gowns; handmade Swiss watches; magnificent handmade chapeaus; solid gold *Romanov* wrist; *Ottoman* ankle bracelets; sable wraps; alligator miniskirts; exotic lingerie and hose; many boxes of obscenely expensive Italian spiked heels; cashmere sweaters; alpaca scarves; and crocodile purses. These and other gifts Prince Markovsky fond and frequently bestowed upon his latest junior dalliance. The clever girl made sure on each occasion receiving the grandee's booty, she then squeal, giggle, shriek, and jabber *witless woman* nonsense to her benefactor's heart's content.

Obeying Mama's instructions to the letter, though, Rolande was meticulous to decline any loan or transfer of cash. She also gracious but firm refused the offer of a rent-free townhouse with accompanying cook, lady's maid, and car. Thus, by preserving her own economic independence and bodily freedom of action, this apprentice Queen of Sheba guaranteed her personal safety just in case Prince Markovsky one day grew possessive or the pair's relationship soured. Rolande had read enough Russian novels to understand that she didn't want to wake up one morning to discover herself now a *kept woman.*

"I wonder if His Grace ever once suspects these quite logical considerations pass through my 'scatterbrained' head?" ventured Rolande, crossing her pretty legs opposite, removing a makeup kit from *Hermes Birkin* handbag.

She answered her own question while repainting her lips. "No, of course, His Grace doesn't! His Grace thinks I'm just 'a stupid woman.'"

The girl soon added, frowning, "I do so wish though, His Grace wouldn't grope me so tight. It hurts! I also so much hate it when he calls me *sweet thing*!" She crossed her pretty legs opposite.

"But then," pondered *Missy*, gazing philosophically at the many historic sites rushing swiftly passed the limousine's bulletproof window, "how else can girls like me and ladies like Grandmother Marie; Great-auntie Bernarde; Mama; Auntie Philippine; Auntie Léonie; and also my cousins Ernestine, Julie, Helene, Claudine, and Francoise ever manage surviving in this world today? What else can we do? Life certainly isn't easy for women with brains!"

The chauffeur made another left.

Now a right.

Then steered directly ahead.

"Of course, brains didn't stop Simone Weil!" piped her young devotee excitedly. "Having brains didn't stop my Simone!" She added, "And no woman in history found herself carrying such a crushing weight of brains as my blessed, sweetest, dearest Simone! And not only was my blessed, sweetest, dearest, so precious Simone forced to contend with that awesome burden of brains, she also needed to somehow manage that heavy load before women in France were permitted to vote!"

No sooner did *Missy* evoke her heroine's name that she cringed with embarrassment. *Shame* was a far better definition of the almost physically painful mental sensation rushing her entire five-foot-six-inch frame.

"But what am *I*, the supposed ardent disciple of an anarchist, labor militant, Spanish loyalist, member of the *Resistance*, great mystic, profound theologian, unacknowledged saint, doing in a prince's stretch limousine! What would my Simone—unappreciated in her own short lifetime, buried in an unmarked grave—think of this supposed admirer's behavior? Not well, that's for certain!"

Rolande chided herself, "What a hypocrite I am! And what a *scatterbrained female, witless woman* hypocrite I am too, if it took this long for me to realize the canyon of difference between who I've always dreamed of emulating and the way I actually conduct my life!"

Despite all those daydreams since age five about her being a warrior storming mighty battlements in the name of justice, freedom, equality, liberty, *Missy* appeared as yet resigned to serve as firm defender of the status quo! As Mama often repeated, "I've passed on to *Missy* all my best genes, all my best *DNA*. I've secured my creation at the head of the social *food chain*, at the top of the class *totem pole*." So much for all her daughter's plans to become a Simone Weil radical!

Unlike her politically-influential, trendsetting mother, Celine, *Missy* harbored no interest in being a regular guest at aristocratic polo and cricket games or of making herself an intimate chum of the continent's rich and powerful. *Missy* didn't hope to reign as absolute monarch of Europe's most exclusive dinner and garden parties. Neither did the girl want a position on television from which she might issue unchallengeable diktats on ladies fashion.

It wasn't as if the prospect of acquiring such lofty social attainments never crossed *Missy*'s fertile, searching young mind. *Divine Right sovereign of ladies couture, tsarina of European style, arbitrator of good taste, empress of a grand historical epoch, the greatest redhead since Queen Elizabeth I*—only saints could resist being periodically drawn to so beckoning a Lorelei! And a saint, Marie-Rolande-Félicitée de Montfort never claimed to be!

"Could you please stop *over there* if you don't mind, Erdal," the young passenger asked the limousine's imposing Turkish liveried chauffeur, fifty hollow-nose bullet clip semiautomatic at driver's belt. "I suddenly feel the need for a breath of early morning fresh air. I also need to exercise my legs."

"As you wish, Mademoiselle Rolande."

The land battleship halted on the left embankment near the Pont Alexandre III. Visible in the distance from one direction was the Grand Palais; from the other, Napoleon's tomb.

The six-thirty morning air was crisp, fresh, invigorating.

"Thank you, Erdal," chattered *Missy*, instinctively adopting a careful studied false persona. "I'll just be a moment. I've suddenly been taken up with one of those silly whims *scatterbrained females* often get. Bless the Virgin none of my vapid number was ever elected president! Imagine the fate of over sixty million French citizens resting in the hands of a vain, hysterical woman! She a creature more worried about missing her next manicure than concerned with achieving world peace! Any time she'd be required delivering an address at a critical summit meeting or need to answer reporters' difficult questions she'd only cry and blubber. She'd quickly make a dreadful embarrassment of the whole nation!"

"Take all the time you need, Mademoiselle Rolande," replied the chauffeur in a voice aloof, disapproving. "I perfectly understand, Mademoiselle Rolande. Females often are overcome by sudden, inexplicable whims."

The second row passenger door opened for her. *Missy* took the chauffeur's arm and exited onto the sidewalk precisely as Mama taught it proper for ladies do so. Following adjustment of her vicuna overcoat and tilt of huge chapeau, she walked to the chest-high embankment wall, soon falling into meditation.

Missy first contemplated the far riverbank. Next, she looked thoughtfully upon the stunning urban vistas provided on her left and right. Finally, she investigated all around.

Time passed.

How much?

Five minutes?

Ten?

Fifteen?

Perhaps more.

So wrapped was *Missy* in introspective thought, she lost track of time.

Gazing long and pensive, she lost the troubles plaguing her young consciousness.

Slipped from her also was a careful studied false persona.

Ooh!" at last the true girl called out in natural voice, gleefully, breaking long silence. "Ooh wee!"

Missy twirled in a merry, unmeddled with, excited, innocent circle.

A girl's entire body, moments earlier weighed down with bitter, painful, rigid self-reproach was now consumed in a strange, free, non-choreographed ecstasy. *Seized* was a more accurate definition.

Once.

Twice.

Three times.

For yet a fourth, fifth roundabout, the prima ballerina gracefully propelled herself. Each succeeding carefree, elegant, happy spin was faster, more joyous than the last.

"Oops, that's so silly of me!"

Not until headgear fell off did the performer at last cease her artful, perfect twirls.

"Awesome!" whispered *Missy*, now in natural, unstudied voice, struggling to fetch her chapeau.

The search required several minutes, as by now, the young lady was thoroughly dizzy. Wobbly on spiked heels; long, fiery red hair tangled, her head was spinning.

Following the elapse of some additional indeterminate time, the racing in head at last abated. Chapeau recovered, *Missy* again surveyed the magnificent urban vista.

She cast inquiring eyes in one direction; next, in a second; then a third; fourth.

The leaping spires of *Gothic* Notre Dame and Sainte Chappelle; the mighty battlements of the medieval Conciergerie; the rambling *Baroque* Louvre museum and Tuilleries Gardens; the *neoclassical* domes of the Invalides and Panthéon; soon too, the Place de Concorde, the Madeleine, Eiffel Tower, Trocadero; from atop Montmartre: the ivory-shaded *Romanesque-Byzantine* Sacre Coeur—all, each both individually and united, became infinitely grander still as a massive canary-yellow sun ascended steadily into a cloudless aquamarine sky.

"Awesome!"

"Awesome! It's awesome!"

"No, really *awesome*!"

"No, really, *really* awesome!"

Missy further adjusted the angle of her massive John Singer Sargent-reminiscent headgear. Last week, Mama, her diktats on haute couture regarded across the continent as infallible, announced on television that it was now the desperate, all-consuming passion of every stylish-European lady to wear *this* particular chapeau. Not surprisingly, the oracle's daughter was the very first to swift fall in sartorial line.

"What a pity!" mused Rolande, gazing on the impressive urban vista. "What a shame views like these available to the eye every day are so routinely ignored by our city's residents! Or at least, so rarely appreciated and given by their spectators the respect and honor these panoramas so richly deserve! Especially that one!" Rolande pointed across the river to a beautiful mural on the wall of a famous museum painted by *Little Marie*. "Especially that splendid picture Mademoiselle Kedari made just before she was assassinated."

Contemplating the scene from all directions, *Missy* suddenly felt ever so small, weak, and insignificant amidst such timeless majesty.

It was a kind of timeless majesty, this dainty viewer increasing sensed to be, like herself, a living, breathing, moving cogitative creature!

Silence thundered.

Quiet roared.

At the same moment, *Missy* experienced the odd sensation of being called forth.

No, *summoned!*

Yes, yes, that was it—*summoned.*

Summoned by the same transcendental forces, first cleansing the girl's mind of all her previous earthbound worry.

Summoned by those same mysterious entities providing this girl a sudden urge to…twirl! To twirl without either Italian spiked heels, opera gown, or vicuna coat obstructing a so graceful, matchless prima ballerina performance.

"Yes, child!" voiceless but loud and clear, sounded the leaping *Gothic* spires of Notre Dame and Sainte Chappelle, so too the medieval battlements of the Conciergerie, the rambling *Baroque* Louvre, the flowering Tuilleries Garden. "Yes, child!" each, all, proclaimed in one united, booming, inaudible confirmation.

These particular monuments were soon endorsed by the Place de Concorde, the Champs d'Elysée, the Arc de Triomphe, Eiffel Tower, and the Trocadero.

All, both, each, and together delivered a message *Missy* recognized to be so unquestionably correct, it needed no words.

"Yes, child," the monuments confided. "It was *you* we summoned! We also were the ones making you happily twirl. Sorry about your chapeau falling off! We'll make sure Mama isn't upset. Perhaps we'll even persuade Mama to praise you during her next television interview."

"Yes, child, we mean *you!*" silent but unmistakably insisted the Madeleine; the Invalides; the Panthéon; the Boulevard Saint Michel; and atop Montmartre, Sacre Coeur. "We summon *you!*"

"Come!" cried unheard to all, save one young individual the grand bridges, the heroic cenotaphs, the wide avenues, and princely homes.

"Follow us, *Missy!*" the historic vistas extolled in unspoken unison.

Their summons was one both monarchical and lovingly intimate.

"Join us, child!" repeated the Timeless Majesty. "It's here where you belong, *sweetheart!* You're meant to be with us! And so one day you eventually will! Maybe not today or tomorrow nor even next month! But you will eventually join us! Don't worry, child. Don't be frightened. No need to rush all at once. Little girls your age have all sorts of other serious and important things to be concerned with."

"Take it all one step at a time, Rolande, dear!" counseled both the wide sky and distant horizon. "Build up your strength, maturity, and momentum as you feel best. We've got patience. We know when you will be fully ready. And then depend on it, Rolande, we will come and make you forever one of our own."

"I can't explain it," whispered *Missy*, overwhelmed. "I just can't explain it." As much as she wished, she was unable, setting her thoughts into better words or welding her ideas into more imaginative sentences.

In a vague, yet no less, clear way, *Missy* also understood herself to be the only person on earth ever privileged to receive this transcendental encounter.

"It's just too awesome to explain. Kinda scary…creepy as well!"

Small, trivial, unimportant *Missy* was…*summoned!*

Summoned to perform a critical role.

Summoned to embrace a noble mission.

One chosen for this girl long before time or the universe even began!

A *mission* absolutely vital, totally irreplaceable for the successful construction of a greater, better, ageless, purer whole!

"They've really chosen little me?" The girl confirmed own question, "Yes, indeed." She was also become conscious that there was no way of escaping the weighty obligation now thrust upon her unsteady adolescent shoulders. "They've r*eally* chosen *little me!*"

Yet precisely when, where, and, above all, *how* was the teenager to accomplish this vital deed?

The Timeless Majesty selecting Rolande to undertake her mission now fallen silent. The answer to her question was painfully uncertain.

Baser Considerations

SCREECH.

A sharp, piercing, high-pitched metallic noise issued from the nearby avenue.

Missy's skin crawled. She sensed her face cringe, arms and legs flinch, heart bolt, spine retract.

The horrible physically painful sound quickly shifted this latter-day Jeanne d'Arc away from the transcendent realm and back into a more tawdry earthbound domain.

"Goodness, gracious me!" cried *Missy*, shifting her eyes away from the cryptic embankment. "Why am I thinking that way about His Grace?"

Never until this morning the girl recognized had she ever made so cool, strategic, emotionally detached, and, above all, mercenary an assessment of her relationship with Prince Markovsky.

"Goodness gracious!"

Celine's daughter felt dreadfully cheap, vulgar, *common*, trashy.

With mounting unease and growing apprehension, she debated if her current role in life might actually be something quite different from what she was raised to assume. Especially so if she was also to prove successful at the weighty mission given her at the summons on the left embankment.

Was *Missy* embracing a historic family *vocation*? Or instead, was she enlisting "as just another second-rate, gold-digging hanger-on?"

Rather than possessed of a lofty *calling*, was she instead preparing to become "just a more refined equivalent of one of those sycophantic lackeys found in the entourage of sexually ambiguous *pop* stars and brawny champion-prize fighters?"

And even if she one day marry the prince, "will I then find myself to be what in the United States is termed *a trophy wife*?" Yes, that vulgar, predatory type of female with dark roots, too much makeup, a push-up bra! One, who increasingly puts expensive white powder up her surgically adjusted nose! That kind of blatant adventuresses who the rightfully dubious relatives and attorney of her new-wealthy *midlife-crisis* groom demand he first obtain a secure prenuptial agreement before the wedding!

"Goodness, gracious! Is that who I ultimately am?"

Cars whizzed by.

Trucks trundled along.

Far above a plane soared in clear turquoise sky.

"Do you think it might now be time we go, Mademoiselle Rolande?" interjected the chauffeur. "Prince Markovsky specifically instructed me, he wants Mademoiselle Rolande delivered home to Madame Celine as soon as possible. Traffic is already beginning to develop, so it's best we leave. You must understand my situation, Mademoiselle Rolande."

"Oh yes, yes, Erdal. I'm terribly sorry!" answered *Missy*, grateful to have her ominous current train of thought broken. "Yes, yes, Erdal. We should go now. I do, of course, well understand your situation."

She eagerly scurried back into the stretch limousine, which then sped off.

Until this singular morning, *Missy* never questioned she possessed a vocation, nor even once doubted she was more than capable of fulfilling that distinguished calling. Like Mama, Auntie Philippine, Auntie Léonie, and all their collective female ancestors for over five centuries, *Missy* believed firmly she was born to be a *Montfort Lady*.

"But is that really, really, true?" she now asked, looking questioningly through the shaded, bulletproof stretch limousine window as palaces, monuments, bridges, and cathedrals fast receded. Great structures that not long before summoned her to fulfill a special mission.

"Well, I can still perform my mission while also being a *Montfort Lady*," insisted Rolande, halting. She never before in need of convincing herself. "That's certainly what Mama and Auntie Philippine and Auntie Léonie will tell me! Mama and Auntie Philippine and Auntie Léonie are all infinitely more perceptive, experienced, and knowledgeable than I can ever hope to be! They realize clearer than I ever will how society operates for girls like us. They're the absolute experts on what makes the world tick for girls like us. They not only understand better than anyone else. They also *show* they understand better than anyone else."

Rolande further admonished to a suddenly doubtful audience of one, "Mama and Auntie Philippine and Auntie Léonie love me. They cherish me, raise me, protect me, hold me warm and close. They always come to me whenever I need them. They know all my desires and all my ambitions, hopes, and dreams before and far better than I know myself."

Missy concluded, only half-convinced, "So who am I? Who am I to presume I've got any right disobeying Mama and Auntie Philippine and Auntie Léonie! Who am, little me, to ever think I've got any right to challenge their authority!"

The girl paused, still deep in worried contemplation.

Yesterday, such assurances would at once set the teenager's mind at ease. Not so the following morning on the left embankment. For the first time in her conscious life, *Missy* was no longer confident in her elders' *better judgment.*

"I wonder if maybe instead..."

Nagging inner doubt, clear evidence of growing maturity, festered unresolved.

That *Missy's* critical self-reassessment should emerge while being driven home in a private limousine from a billionaire's fabulous estate— she clothed in queenly chapeau, vicuna overcoat, long alpaca scarf, magnificent silk opera gown, $700 Italian stiletto heels, *mogul-period* diamonds in hair and around neck, *Safavid Dynasty* Persian rubies on earlobes and fingers, solid-gold *Romanov Ottoman* bracelets on wrists and ankles, her manicured hands inside exclusive-boutique sable gloves clutching *Hermes Birkin* handbag— contained initially for "all Mama's best genes and *DNA*" no irony. Only upon reaching No. 3 Rue Artemis half an hour later and observing her snappy reflection in the full-length mirror of her bedroom's walk-in closet did the satire at last register in the girl's consciousness.

"Oh my God!" screamed *Missy* with horror. "I'm not carrying out a mission! I'm being an *adventuress*! My God, I'm an adventuress, an *adventuress*!"

Who Am I Really?

ROLANDE NEEDN'T TROUBLE HER tender, idealistic heart. She was no more an *adventuress* than any of her historic, distinguished Montfort ancestors.

She was becoming a...*courtesan.*

Upon graduating from novice to full member of this ancient order, "Mama's best genes, best *DNA*" would likely consider the immense social privileges, wide indirect political/economic influence she came to personally enjoy and subtly exercise, mere proper compensation. It all a well-earned reward for devoting an entire life to providing invaluable assistance to "fools with trousers." A form of critical support she was required contributing, totally unacknowledged. For in addition to frequent service of a physical, emotional nature, a courtesan must also formulate, engineer, set in motion the entire strategy by which her gentlemen achieve worldly distinction. And a courtesan is obliged accomplishing it all while at the same time making sure these gentlemen remain convinced her shrewd woman's counsel is really their own brilliant male idea.

As Mama famously scolded journalists disapproving of her notoriety, "You men have nothing to complain about. You're still always going to be the one on top!"

If still too young to originate strategies for men to take credit, her present relationship with Markovsky just a training exercise, *Missy* nonetheless already demonstrated she clearly possessed "all Mama's best genes and best *DNA*." It might even be argued, gentlemen should already start providing a small advance on the tremendous amount they would surely owe this immensely talented girl in years to come.

Yet, should Rolande eventually be unwilling to perpetuate the family tradition, how else then could she engage the world? Do so in a manner allowing her to one day die assured humanity was better off, or at least not worse than when she first found it? If not as a courtesan, how else could Rolande fulfill her existential summons on the embankment? The solution wasn't easy to discover. After all, she couldn't search for the answer where most girls do.

Daughters shouldn't be educated, insists the collective perceived wisdom of rarefied, self-perpetuating, elite European society. *Education only spoils a daughter's natural tenderness, ruins her usual fresh, warm, compliant spirit. Giving a daughter an education—a boys' education, that is—serves simply to jam her impressionable little brain with all kinds of* concepts, theories and notions.

Education can also result in nasty trouble later on, warns centuries of accumulated, sacred, cultural heritage. *Sending daughters to school only makes them want to wear trousers, cut their hair short, and talk back! Next, they'll want a* career, *want to be* fulfilled. *They'll smoke marijuana; become atheists, lesbians, communists, hippies; end up marrying one of those morose leftist intellectuals from NYU who never shut up about the Tonkin Gulf Resolution, Watergate, or Donald Trump! Can you image Marie-Rolande-Félicitée de Montfort from the rich, exclusive, historic kingmaker, 7th arrondissement of Paris, suddenly reduced to Mrs. Sheldon Jabotinsky of Rivington Street, New York City? She then bearing children with names like Harmony, Flowers, Essence?*

Or even worse, cautions hallowed, unquestionable, aristocratic social custom, *Israelites, at least, don't filch the silverware, imagine the sweetheart moving in with some criminal sex-obsessed, dope-intoxicated Negro! One who soon abandons the dear pregnant, needle in arm, white powder up her nose, penniless in Harlem! You don't want your grandchildren to be part-Negro, do you? They'll be given names like Tyrone, Dexter, Aisha! Frizzy hair, big lips, yellowish complexion half breeds! Not one, not the other! Then eventually, Tyrone or Dexter will start wearing a bow tie, call himself Jamal, and drive a jet into a skyscraper! Won't that do wonders for France's standing abroad! It's enough to make you support abortion! No, no, it's far better giving a daughter a good, strict, traditional upbringing. It's all she's required to learn in order to play her proper role in proper society. In time, she'll understand, fully agree, and thank her parents in the end. Just watch! It's precisely how she'll insist on raising her own daughter!*

"No, *Missy*! And that's final!" echoed Celine one soft afternoon five years earlier. Countess de Montfort is certainly no anti-Semite or racist. "No, you can't go to school."

The pretty duo was then seated in the first floor *Louis XV-style* parlor of *Baroque* No. 3 Rue Artemis. Painted-fired *Han* and *Tang Dynasty* china vases nearby were filled with roses, hydrangeas, rhododendrons, orchids, salvias, crocus, tulips, and delphiniums. That day had also been the only time Rolande ever managed, gathering enough courage, to even vaguely refer to a strictly taboo subject. Tone of Mama's reply announced the matter was already long resolved. Her answer also warning the child might raise the dreadful issue again only if she prepared to instantly receive several well-deserved smacks on tender young fanny.

"Besides," elaborated Celine, melodic voice growing maternal, protective, "see how easily my *Missy* picked up *seven* foreign languages at home simply by listening to Mama's gentlemen chums! Most daughters your age are too busy worshiping sexually ambiguous *rock* players. I won't insult the word *musicians*. Most daughters your age are obsessed, idolizing dark-roots movie stars or too-many-muscles-to-be-natural athletes with no sense in their thick skulls. By contrast, *Missy's* heroine is Simone Weil! Look at all those deep theological issues you brought up when I was teaching you *catechism*? Even Cardinal Blanchard said he couldn't dispute the positions you took! 'She's a splendid child,' His Eminence told me. 'What a wise little lady you've created, Madame de Montfort!'" Mama pledged. "So there's no need my *Missy* ever look beyond her home for enlightenment!"

From the portraits on the salon's finely-papered walls, earlier historic *Montfort ladies* signaled their five-and-a-half centuries' agreement.

"*Proper* daughters are kept at home," illuminated Celine, she, dressed in parakeet blue, crossing her legs opposite. "You and Ferdinande are *proper* daughters. You both must be kept at home."

Parent instructed, "Now stand up and let me fix your frock."

"Yes, Mama," Rolande instantly complied.

"Let Mama see to it so her treasure looks like a *proper* young Christian lady." Celine explained, refastening the buttons on Rolande's short-patterned dress, then adjusting the hem of offspring's outfit. "Education isn't good for girls like us. In fact, *Missy*, an innocent, simple soul like you should never be allowed anywhere near a school. Education will spoil you completely! It will take away your so warm, sincere, engaging spirit! The only thing 'education' will succeed in doing is to fill your unique, brilliant, but far-too-impressionable brain with all men's socialist *concepts*; mercenary *theories*; narcissistic, self-pitying, conceited *notions*! School, or what men say we're supposed to believe is *school*, will destroy all that's so beautiful and wonderful in your little sweet, noble, unmeddled-with head! All having you *educated* will accomplish is make you want to wear trousers, cut your hair short, smoke marijuana, learn unladylike language! School, or what men say we're supposed to believe is *school*, will make you stop going to Mass, stop going to confession, no longer desire assisting in the Altar Guild. Why, you'll even stop believing in God! Terrible! Abominable! No, no, Mama won't ever allow that fate happening to either you or Ferdinande."

She guaranteed, "Anyway, the only things *proper* daughters ever need to know, their Mama, another *daughter*, one speaking from personal experience, not just from the other sex's grandiose philosophy, can teach far better at home. And also, my priceless *Missy* doesn't need worrying her little head over *school* with all those big, thick famous books she's collecting upstairs. It must be a regular library now! Time will come when it's celebrated as the *Missy* Collection or as the *Missy* Library."

Celine advised, "Besides, there will be no one at *school* Mama can depend on to keep her *Missy's* frock straight!" She gave Rolande an affectionate, maternal pat on bottom, then, motioned her child sit down, again. "So many scholarly, learned, sophisticated books my *Missy* has! What's the number grown too? Mama's lost count! Maybe you'll need cataloging them all soon. Under certain conditions, Mama just might possibly be persuaded permitting you to become a librarian. What's that newest in the series of biographies of famous, noble-hearted ladies Mama instructed sweetheart to read? The volume arriving just yesterday by special post?"

"The Life of Jeanne d'Arc."

"Ah yes, *The Life of Jeanne d'Arc*. An excellent, uplifting, inspirational subject! Especially appropriate for you to concentrate your thoughts upon! In the crude Americanized world we sadly find ourselves confronting. It's a terrible shame we don't have Jeanne d'Arc to rescue us today! Perhaps maybe we also don't deserve to have her." Then after pause, she said, "My birthday is May 4, remember?"

"Yes, of course, I do, Mama!"

"Well," responded Celine, smiling gleeful, "my *Missy* will discover in the newest biography of a famous lady I purchased for her that May 4, 1429, is the day our little Jeanne opened the attack on Orléans. The silly, old, incompetent male generals didn't want to follow a teenage girl. They didn't believe a teenage girl could ever know anything about military strategy, tactics, commanding an army or being a leader of men. Well, our little Jeanne certainly wasn't bothered by their grumbling. She soon proved the stupid old fogies wrong! Didn't she, *Missy*?"

"That's right, Mama! Jeanne soon sent those arrogant Brits packing!"

"Afterward, the stupid men, originally thinking our little Jeanne's plan wouldn't work, tried stealing the credit! But no one paid them any attention! They knew it was our little Jeanne's strategy, and it was our little Jeanne's victory and her triumph alone! And that was only one small part of the peasant girl's inspiring story. On my birthday too! Not that Mama will ever permit her child joining the army or associating with rough characters, of course! Nor does Mama wish her child hearing voices, even if they're the voices of saints and angels! Nor does Mama wish seeing *Missy* burnt at the stake."

"Oh no, I promise!"

"Good."

"Mama was kept at home. She never attended *school*," recounted Celine, refastening the straps on daughter's high heels. "Do you think your sweet, kind, affectionate, grandmother Marie, your dear auntie Philippine and auntie Léonie would be the noble, selfless, Christian examples all must seek to emulate if they were...*educated*?"

Celine next motioned Rolande to contemplate the pairs' illustrious feminine ancestors gracing the salon's four papered walls. Some of these portraits were painted by Durer, Holbein, Breughal, Cranach, Vermeer, Rembrandt. Others (some with the lady in the nude) were contributed by Van Dyck, Poussin, Claude Lorrain, Reynolds, Gainsborough, David, Goya, Gericault, Ingres, Manet, Courbet, Cezanne, Klimt. More recent images (some again, with the lady in the nude) were crafted by Picasso, Matisse, Braque, Modigliani, Laurencin, Rivera, and Kokoschka.

"Madame de Pompadour didn't go to *school*!" reminded Celine, now brushing Rolande's long, thick fiery red locks. "Theodora captured Justinian without ever going to *school*. Roxelana held sway over Suleiman the Magnificent and the whole Ottoman Empire without ever going to *school*. Aspasia, Diane of Poitiers, Gabrielle d'Estrée, Barbara Villers, Lola Montez, Belle Otero didn't receive an *education*. Our kind still manages throughout history, accomplishing more than a few noteworthy things in this man's always-on- top world, do we not! So indeed too will, *Missy*! Trust me!"

Parent soon added, "Mama always knows best. Likely, no, definitely, she knows her pondering treasure will accomplish something more lofty, more noble, grand than all the previous five hundred and fifty years of *Montfort Ladies* put together!"

She pecked Rolande on right cheek, pressed her daughter's hand affectionately. "So from this day forth, sweetheart, promise Mama there will be absolutely no more of this wanting to go to *school* nonsense."

"Yes, I promise, Mama!" pledged Rolande earnestly. "From this day forth, there will be no more of this wanting to go to *school* nonsense! Girls like us don't go to silly *school*."

Celine's views might seem peculiar given her life story. However, they shouldn't and not simply because human beings are, by nature, enigmas. For over five hundred and fifty years in every generation, our own included popes. princes, theologians, paramount statesmen, generals, admirals, diplomats, foreign ministers, novelists, scientists, dramatists, poets, composers, painters, sculptors—all sought, still seek, the untutored *Montfort Ladies* to resolve their complex self-inflicted male dilemmas. Given this fact, as Celine and all her family's mothers logically conclude, education is vastly overrated!

If for all men's prestigious university degrees, scholarly prizes, learned attainments, they still remain unable to succeed without an "ignorant" woman's constant encouragement, the gents' formal education definitely isn't worth much! Hopelessly clouded as are men's fragile minds with *concepts*, *theories*, and *notions*, only "unlettered, naïve, cowardly" women possess the intellectual capacity, wisdom, and courage to lead humanity forward! Herself often called upon to rescue men from their education, Celine was confident of what she spoke. As a loving, devoted parent, she'd be terribly remiss letting Rolande be exposed to what popular fad misnames—*school.*

The Missy Collection

SO THEN, IF NOT an adventuress, what on earth else am I possibly qualified to be? wondered Rolande after she was delivered home in Prince Markovsky's sleek, shiny, feline black stretch limousine the morning following *Carmen. So what do I do with myself?*

Her near exact contemporary in age, Middle-Eastern artist and political refugee Pascale Kedari created frescoes speedily recognized across Europe as masterpieces. The young *Messenger's* ingenious strokes of paint on wet plaster recently inspired a historic, social, cultural, and political movement (some said, a revolution). If Rolande too, immensely gifted, her own talent was not for visual art.

"So if not a painter, what am I to be instead?"

Celine's daughter delicately removed her new vicuna coat and secured it on a firm wooden hanger. Next, *Missy* placed the garment in a spot of honor, all its very splendid, magnificent, own within large walk-in closet. Impressive new jewelry she placed with equal care in an ornate metal, ivory, upholstered box atop a tall, auburn-colored, lacquered walnut *Queen Anne* chest of drawers with shiny brass handles. She locked the box shut. A framed lithograph by Daumier hung on the papered wall directly above.

"So what am I supposed to do instead?"

Missy took off her beautiful silk strapless turquoise opera gown and rested it on another large, thick, wooden hanger near the vicuna coat. Next, taking off white heels, wriggling out of pantyhose, she wrapped her lovely five-foot-four-inch, well-endowed feminine body in a colorful, decorated Japanese kimono. Finally, climbing atop a dark-oak four-poster canopied bed, she once more questioned herself aloud, "So what am I supposed to do?"

She lay across the mattress, her torso remaining semi-erect, supported by hands placed behind back. The bed was originally constructed for a person much taller. Its current occupant's pretty legs reached nowhere near the front. Bare feet twitching repeatedly hinted at extensive adolescent reflection and anxiety.

Hoping to obtain the answer to dilemma, Rolande shifted on her side so that she might better survey the walls of the other half of her large combination study and bedroom. Mama was absolutely correct: her younger daughter was amassing a regular library, one now in clear need of cataloging! Publications small and large, thick and narrow, tall or short completely covered three walls from dark-wood paneled floor to high-frescoed ceiling. A sliding wooden ladder attached to a steel pole running the room just beneath ceiling enabled a reader to easily get her hands on the books in the distant top shelves. The letters *RM* in Gothic script stamped on a copper plate over the bottom wheels were the initials of the company building it, not those of the book collector.

How many weighty volumes, academic tomes, bound periodicals were there now? That was difficult to say. Their owner long ago lost count.

Missy began acquiring books almost from the moment she first learned to read at age four. These works were written not just in her native French but also over time in all seven foreign languages she became fluent—English, German, Italian, Greek, Farsi, Latin, and Arabic.

If a few of these impressive works were given as birthday or Christmas presents, the vast majority were purchased by *Missy* on her diligent, genteel feminine own. The very first one she bought, when her head still hadn't yet reached the top of the merchant's front counter. Some titles *Missy* obtained in regular bookstores or at museum gift shops. Others were ordered over the Internet, found at flea markets, or located at church bazaars. Still, additional acquisitions she discovered while rummaging through the old green or gray mettle stalls running parallel the embankment.

This last source was often the most fruitful. Sometimes, when searching along the Seine, *Missy* felt like a great archeologist. She imagined being Heinrich Schliemann discovering ancient Troy or Sir Howard Carter locating the tomb of Tutankhamen. During one of these excavations, *Missy* unearthed at the bottom of a huge pile of dusty old tomes, all five volumes of an original 1863 edition printing of Francois Guizot's *History of France*. On another digging, for so here the term "digging" was quite applicable, she found the philosopher Auguste Comte's 1841 original treatise on what he chose to call *Postivism*. Judged by the shocking cheap prices, the seller obviously didn't have the foggiest notion of what he offered.

For an instant, *Missy* was seized by a pang of guilt, felt deeply ashamed at the thought of exploiting this unforeseen opportunity. Just for a second however. The dainty explorer soon remembered that "He"—or in this case, *she*—"who hesitates is lost." So much for all of her mama and aunties' religious instruction! Comte and Guizot, both fiercely secular authors, would have readily approved this young bibliophile's final decision.

From atop the oak canopied bed, a pair of inquisitive young gray-green feminine eyes raced left to right across the long shelves of books and bound periodicals. A sticker printed in the observer's own handwriting taped above one crowded shelf announced a far-too-loose category: "*Nonfiction.*"

Complete Works of Simone Weil, *The Black Death*, *Christian Symbolism in Medieval Art*, Averroes, Saladin, Dr. Livingstone, Margaret of Anjou, *The Thirty Years War*, Krakatoa, Polybius, Schopenhauer, Justinian and Theodora, Hume, *History of Venice*, *The Abbesses of Fontrevault*, *Romanesque Architecture*, Marie Curie, Catherine the Great, Descartes, *Sheep Raising*, *Excavation of Troy*, Tocquevill, Giotto, Montaigne, *German Expressionism*, Wittgenstein, St. Augustine, *Hegel*, Locke, Hobbes, Alcuin, Kierkegaard, *The Upanishads*, *Secret Diary of Harold Ickes*, *The Wars of the Roses*...

Her reading of the titles on that particular shelf at last done, the collector's attention swift umped to another row of publications. This time, the handwritten sticker announcing the category of volumes had long ago vanished. Again, inquisitive adolescent feminine eyes sped left to right.

Animal Husbandry, St. Therese of Lisieux, *Knight Heraldry,* Akhmatova, *Taoism,* Blanche of Castile, Milton, Flaubert, *Medieval Arabic Poetry,* Rousseau, Shakespeare, Wordsworth, Verlaine, Paul Claudel, *The Brothers Karamazov,* Anne Frank, Turgenev, Cretien de Troyes, J. S. Mill, St. Thomas Aquinas, Keats, *Paintings of Turner,* Henry VIII, Elizabeth I, *Lost Illusions,* Livy, Tacitus, Marie de France, *Buddhism, The Red and the Black,* Newton, Pasteur, *Greek Mythology, Mother Goose,* Rimbaud, Camille Claudel, Baudelaire, *Bird Watching,* Hugo, *The Suffragettes, The History of Fashion…*

That section done, the observer next turned to a third long shelf of weighty tomes. This section vaguely labeled "*Great Ideas*"

Buddenbrooks, Tristan and Iseult, Eleanor of Aquitaine, Ronsard, *The Iliad,* Dean Acheson, Petrarca, *Dairies Today, History of Persia,* Gladstone, *Stained Glass,* Cicero, *Muslim Astronomers,* Hildegard of Bingen, Plato, Caedmon, Dante, Walter Benjamin, Boccaccio, Galileo, Fourier, Chaucer, Nietzsche, Burke, Marx, Thucydides, *Tess of the d'Urbervilles,* Herodotus, Captain Cook, *The Spanish Civil War,* Darwin, Francis of Assisi, Christine de Pizan, Marcuse, Disraeli, Herder, Kleist, Feuerbach, *Roosevelt and Hopkins,* Jaspers, Humboldt, *Poetry of Sister Juana Ines de la Cruz…*

"Good Lord!" cried *Missy,* abruptly breaking off her survey. "I'm only an awesome *scatterbrained female*! I'm only an awesome dilettante! I'm just one of those characters who can say words like 'zeitgeist,' 'gemeinschaft' and 'weltanschauung,' one who can rattle off a lot of names and dates yet, in the end, doesn't really know anything!"

The young bibliophile declared, "Ultimately, I'm not learned at all!" She looked away, painfully embarrassed. "I'm not smart! I'm only a… *silly*! I'm only an awesome…*silly*!"

Feeling immensely ashamed, the girl rolled up into a ball. She wept desperately until physical exhaustion at last brought welcomed sleep.

Missy needn't fear. This pretty auto-diktat, attractive polymath was no *scatterbrained female,* nor was she a "*silly*" any more than were Diane of Poitiers, Madame de Pompadour, or Madame de Stael. In fact, although she lacking formal education, Mama's Treasure completely on her exceptional own initiative became a superb little scholar, a true *Renaissance Girl*. Rolande was one of the best-read persons in all Europe, likely, on any continent! Everyone claiming to be an "intellectual" knows of Adam Smith's *The Wealth of Nations*, can recognize the names Goethe's *Faust*, Kant's *Critique of Pure Reason*, *Essay on the Principle of Population* by Malthus, Freud's *Interpretation of Dreams*, and *The Meditations* of Marcus Aurelius. But how many besides "ignorant," "uneducated," "silly" Rolande, actually read them? And read them all in the author's original language too!

Even if the vast store of knowledge she accumulated since age four was now amassed in a monstrous hodgepodge, it still provided Rolande a far clearer, far more discerning perception of the world than over 95 percent of the entire human race. What she did lack, however, was the certainty of where precisely to direct her immense, unique, mental strengths and powerful spiritual abilities. Her next encounter with Prince Markovsky still a week away, Rolande did all possible during the intervening days to decipher and unravel the great mystery, to discover why Timeless Majesty chose summoning this particular s*weet thing* on the embankment.

I

"So where is my scholarly *Missy* off to this time?*"* queried Celine fondly, seated graceful in cherrywood red damask armchair and dressed in a short parakeet-blue skirt; white frilly blouse with three buttons undone, revealing ample cleavage; splendid legs crossed and wearing white heels. The latest edition of *La Croix* was folded in ladylike hands. A sudden, living, cognizant burst of light from an ascendant 10:00 a.m. sun entered through a gently opened French window to the left. Rays from heaven illuminated much of the first floor *Louis XV-style* salon in Madame de Montfort's *Baroqu*e Parisian townhouse.

"I'm off to discover who I really am, Mama," informed Rolande, enigmatic as she approached the dark-stained oak front door. A serious, thoughtful expression was on her determined teenage face.

"Aha!" responded Celine, asking no more. Like every p*roper* female parent, she instinctively knew beforehand all the details of her child's latest endeavor. "Well, I hope you locate what you're after, my junior Aristotle."

Turning the page of the official French Roman Catholic national daily, Celine announced, "When you eventually come back from your expedition, love, you must definitely read the most recent speech Cardinal Blanchard delivered at the French Academy. It's what you children call 'awesomely interesting.' It's just the kind of subject my *Missy* so very much enjoys."

"I promise to read it, Mama."

"Mama knows her *Missy* will. Now go have fun, if under the current circumstances, 'fun' is the appropriate word."

Reflection

DOWN ONE QUIET, POSH, chestnut tree-lined residential Parisian street walked young Mademoiselle de Montfort, deep in thought.

Steady click, click, click of her high heels unaltered, she soon proceeded along yet another charming urban path; later, a third, a fourth, fifth, sixth, seventh.

Click, click, click, click.

Running parallel all the way to both left and right, as if offering the philosophic girl shielding, maternal protection, was an unbroken series of near-uniform four-story eighteenth-century light-brown townhouses. Each possessed a similar black wrought-iron gate and almost identical tall, polished, thick wooden front door with polished brass handles. Each succeeding townhouse boasted a set of wide ornate *French windows,* all shuttered and visually alike. Vehicles not parked outside, no easy indication was given as to whether these stately homes were currently occupied.

Click, click, click, click of contemplative high heels.

After sojourning here for roughly an hour, Rolande exited this discreet, upscale residential neighborhood and navigated a wide, much more frequented public square.

No less consumed in silent debate, she crossed a hectic, noisy avenue.

Reaching the far side, the genteel young stroller made a left.

Following a later right turn, she traveled straight ahead.

Click, click, click, click.

A soft, restful, comforting breeze was in the air.

The temperature was perfect.

No clouds obstructed a boundless Delft-blue sky.

On, on, on, the girl walked in intense meditation.

Click, click, click, click.

Every day that week, Rolande took an extended, thoughtful jaunt through various streets and neighborhoods of Paris.

Her present expedition passed through the semi-enclosed Tuilleries Gardens with its shaded gravel paths, marble statues, and great water fountain at the center. Adjacent west of the Louvre, south of Rue Rivoli, this park was in brief walking distance of the right embankment.

Click, click, click, click.

Spring was bursting forth in all colorful, confident earnest. Red, blue, green, white, yellow, orange, pink, violet, purple profusions of roses, amaryllis, dahlias, clematis, orchids, lilies, cornflowers, begonias, crocus, anemones, cosmos tulips, peonies, and hyacinths welcomed Rolande's so observant adolescent eyes.

Entering from the east, she recited, as was her habit, the beautiful melancholy words of Omar Khayyam.

> *Sometimes I think that never blows so red the rose/ as where some dying Caesar bled/ and every hyacinth the garden wears/ dropped in her lap from some once lovely head.*

After stopping at a Renoir-painting-reminiscent refreshment stand to purchase a red cherry ice, Rolande sat down to enjoy the treat atop a green park bench.

Just ahead was an ocean of bright, young, vibrant, semi-cognizant, multicolored flowers in a historic well-tended garden. It boasted magnificent dahlias, amaryllis, orchids, cornflowers, lilies, begonias, crocus, anemones, cosmos, tulips, peonies, roses, and hyacinths. Before the eye were undulating waves of red, white, blue, orange, pink, and yellow.

Tourists snapped photos.

Lovers communed.

Squirrels raced up chestnut and plane trees.

A flock of lavender birds near the spraying neoclassical fountain took flight.

Children noisily scampered a large gravel circular path, nannies pleading to no avail their little charges slow down.

All the while deep in thought as she enjoyed too the sinfully delicious cherry ice, Rolande struggled to find the answer for which she yearned.

The last drop of that marvelous, tasty cherry ice finally traveled, as Mama would say, "down my *Missy's* Little Red Lane," the girl stood up, a worried expression on her cute face.

"It seems the answer won't be found here," conceded Rolande in a troubled, preoccupied whisper. She readjusted the angle of her chapeau. Next, she searched for her lace handkerchief placed in a *Hermes Birkin* handbag. "At least the answer I'm after won't be found here today."

Tourist boats glided lackadaisically the river.

Flags of primary colors floated majestically over *Baroque* palaces.

A sweet, memorable fragrance was to be inhaled.

Summoned abruptly on the left embankment, Rolande hoped this stroll through her favorite stomping ground might provide crucial detail about the existential mission Timeless Majesty selected for her to fulfill.

Debating the issue first from a military perspective, *Commander in Heels* recognized she could direct her troops far more efficiently, win her campaign swifter, capture the mighty enemy citadel much sooner if she first given instructions on what was precisely expected of her. Was she to just seize the battlefield and then withdraw or, instead, permanently occupy the territory she'd taken? Could she engage allies? Call in reinforcements if necessary? Was she expected to hold the high ground or the riverbank no matter what the cost? Or should need arise, she be allowed to conduct a tactical retreat in order to regroup, resupply her divisions?

Did the fetching young general possess the authority to independently set peace terms over her defeated foe or must she first wait for word from home? The first alternative was much preferable. Time is fleeting, sometimes all too fleeting. Victories should be taken advantage of, exploited to the fullest—and at the speediest! No need losing valuable extra, unforeseen opportunities through needless delay. "He,"—or rather *she*—"who hesitates is lost!" History is shaped by those men, or sometimes even *women*, with courage to dare, seize the moment, grab destiny by the throat, and bend it to one's own will! That's the way to go. The way it's supposed to go!

Few things worry commanders more than vague, incomplete orders. Having read several books about the Crimean War, Rolande knew the disastrous *Charge of the Light Brigade* was caused by Lord Cardigan receiving only vague, incomplete orders. This girl had no intention of also dashing headlong into cannons, even if only figurative ones!

"It seems the answer I seek won't be found here today," repeated Rolande in a troubled, preoccupied whisper. "At least not this morning, at least I don't think so."

After first being so talkative, so kind and engaging, Timeless Majesty had now grown capriciously silent. If so swift in calling upon Rolande to embrace her new duty, those same divine, otherworldly forces were now become curiously unhelpful in explaining precisely what the girl's new duty entailed!

"Still reaching for the ultimate *Why*, still in quest of the supreme *Because*...Rolande, my favorite scholar, my dearest philosopher," suddenly interjected older half sister, Ferdinande de Godefroy, approaching from behind. The pretty newcomer wore a lovely, designer, tailored, not off-the-rack short dress, spiked heels, sheerest pantyhose, wide chapeau. She also clutched proprietary the left arm of the Duc d'Aveyron, director of the World Bank.

"Wonderful to see you again, Ferdinande!" exclaimed Rolande with delight. "*See*, Ferdinande." She pointed to the pair's identical massive headgear. "*See*, Ferdinande! *See*! It's just like yours! We both must've listened to Mama's latest television interview. We both must've heard Mama declare that every fashionable lady must wear this particular bonnet! As her daughters, we both naturally wasted no time in following Mama's order!" *Missy* performed a graceful, matchless pirouette. "Am

64

I wearing my chapeau just as instructed, Ferdinande? Have I got it on correctly? Am I wearing it at the angle that all ladies must?"

Countess de Montfort's heiress apparent as European fashion oracle, no one was presently in a better position than Ferdinande de Godefroy to answer her little sister's plea.

"You're wearing it perfectly, Rolande! You look splendid! Magnificent!"

"Bless you, bless you, Ferdinande, dear!"

"Thank you, dear."

If, like all *Montfort ladies*, each was blessed with striking good looks, beautiful legs, easy aristocratic deportment, these two particular members of the famous clan obviously shared just one parent. Like Celine, Rolande was five feet six. However, she was a redhead not a cherry blonde and bore almost no facial resemblance to Mama. Ferdinande de Godefroy, in contrast, while possessing Mama's same color hair and almost identical face, was only four foot ten. The Duc d'Aveyron, whose arm she clutched, proprietary, towered far above at six foot six.

"It's ever so nice seeing you again, Ferdinande, dear!" piped Rolande, ecstatic.

This was *Missy's* first encounter with her older half-sibling in over a year. All the sad thoughts created by their long separation vanished as if never occurred.

"I didn't expect this! Certainly not today!" cried the younger of lovely duo. "What an awesome treat! How long has it been since we met last, Ferdinande, dear? We keep earnestly making dates by telephone or letter to meet over lunch, to hold hands, to reminisce about old times, have really good giggles together. We really mean it each time, don't we?"

"Yes, we certainly do, Rolande, dearest!"

"Every time we set a date to meet, we chatter on the telephone daily during the week before for nearly an hour. We each go to the beauty parlor to get our hair fixed up, we each chose our favorite outfit and newest pair of heels to wear—but then something always happens! Prince Markovsky insists he needs me or you're suddenly asked to be hostess at some big event and just can't get out of it—that kind of thing. Seems the gods are against us. Well, anyway, at last we meet again. And by surprise too! That's even better, even more awesome! Guess that just as once before, the fates can't keep us apart forever!"

Soon Rolande added with touch of concern, "Have you been here long? Think of it!" She giggled with mock self-reproach. "Me, all this time just strutting about like I'm someone important! Me behaving like a *silly* all that time, not even noticing you were here!"

"Oh for a minute or two," responded her older half sister gently, pecking Rolande's red-painted lips. "Don't worry! It was ever so nice watching your serious deliberations. Was it not so, Your Grace?" Ferdinande de Godefroy turned to her famous, distinguished lover. She clutched the nobleman's left harm tight, proprietary, rubbed her soft cheek against Aveyron's arm like a cat leaving its scent upon a hard-won possession so as no doubt could arise as to this valued object's unquestioned ownership.

The director of the *World Bank* nodded in sincere agreement. "So indeed, Mademoiselle Rolande!" he commented. "I've often heard you mentioned by my possessive Ferdinande. It's good to receive an opportunity we can at last cross paths!"

A little girl in polka dots toddled by in pursuit of pink ball.

Silver-hued jet fighter voyaged Delft sky far above.

Gray dog barked.

"His Grace and I were strolling in this direction when I glimpsed you by chance," elaborated Ferdinande de Godefroy.

Each half sister took a few moments to admire the others set of lower limbs. Both young ladies gratefully acknowledged the compliment she received by issuing her impressed observer a knowing smile and an understanding wink of eyes.

"I saw you, as I said, grasping for the ultimate *Why*. Immediately, I told the Duc d'Aveyron, 'See. *See*, Your Grace, see that meditative girl atop the green bench—the one with all the massive red hair going every which way? That's Rolande, my half sister. She's such a noble, scholarly, brilliant dear.'"

Ferdinande de Godefroy explained to the great financier. "She's not a *scatterbrained female* like me. Rolande's as smart as any man! I used to tease her, saying, 'God must've been interrupted in the middle of His work by some other important business and forgot you were supposed to be a boy!' You ought to look at all the men's books, all the books on men's subjects, men's issues Rolande has accumulated, Your Grace! Mama needed to have new shelves constructed because the original old ones were practically giving way from all the weight."

Continued her stylish older half sister, "And Rolande read them all too! Well, no, actually she'll never read them all because more weighty learned tomes keep on coming to her each month in the mail! Lots of people know the names of famous books, but Rolande's actually read them! Some more than once! And in the original language! They're all far too long and complicated for a *scatterbrain* like me. Rolande understands more about —*isms*, is better acquainted with —*ians*, she's finer versed when it comes to —*ists*, —*ites, neo*—*s* than anyone you'll ever come across. She's a regular library in a skirt! For all those interested in epochs and ages, *pre*—*s* and —*post*s, she's the one to consult! Rolande is as smart as any man! Any two, three, or even four, five, six, ten men put together!"

Ferdinande de Godefroy quickly added, her anxious glowing praise of her younger half sister's intellect alone might be misinterpreted as a veiled criticism of sibling's physical appearance or taste in fashion. "Of course, Rolande is also *really* cute! She always wears *really* cute outfits! Rolande has ever so sexy legs too! Not many other women can get away with wearing such a short skirt—and also while at Mass! But you, Rolande dear, you're practically supposed to wear a skirt that short. Say, where did you ever get that terrific color heels? They're tremendous!"

"Thank you so much, Ferdinande, dear" replied *Missy*, both grateful and reassuring. "Thank you so much, Ferdinande precious. I think you've got ever so sexy legs too! Not many women can get away with wearing such a short skirts! But you, well, you're practically supposed to wear one that short! So nice you like my heels too. I'd love to show where you bought them, show where I too can buy a pair."

"Anyway," Ferdinande de Godefroy resumed her tale, "I said to the Duc d'Aveyron, 'Let's go and watch Rolande for a while closer, Your Grace. Let's watch her deliberations. Follow her quest to confront *the grand scheme of things*, my sister's effort to grab *the meaning of life* by the lapels. Such a good, inspiring, otherworldly girl she is, Your Grace! She's as smart as any man!'"

Rolande looked away embarrassed, flattered being judged as smart as any man.

"No need to be so modest, Rolande, dear," implored Ferdinande de Godefroy, again grasping her lover's arm, proprietary. "You're much to be admired in this vulgar, materialistic, Americanized I'll-wait-till-the-movie-comes-out world. We need more lofty, energetic spirits like you! Anyway, at last, I thought it both important and only polite to speak."

"It's awesome for us to meet Ferdinande, dear, *really* awesome! I mean it."

"I do too!"

The two girls pecked their red-painted lips.

"Ooh! Ooh!" shouted two young fashion plates in refined unison. "Ooh! Ooh!"

Obligingly, the Duc d'Aveyron pried himself loose of his mistress's grip and took a few steps backward so he might allow the sisters to jabber, giggle, and jump up and down in each other's arms with all ladylike ferocity. At least to the extent their high heels and short hems permitted.

"Ooh, ooh, ooh, ooh, Ferdinande!"

"Ooh, ooh, ooh, ooh Rolande!"

Wide chapeaus soon fell to the ground, long red and cherry blond hair covered two attractive faces. The girls squealed happily. They squealed still happily more.

"Ooh! Ooh! Ooh! Ooh!"

A little lady in polka dots toddled back, her pink ball retrieved.

Squirrels darted by.

Birds in tree branches chirped.

Celine's two daughters at last released warm embrace, each out of breath, their jewelry askew. The Duc d'Aveyron, who in the meantime retrieved the duo's headgear, returned each large, wide chapeau to its owner graciously.

Ferdinande de Godefroy again snatched her lover's arm, proprietary.

"Little Blondie always wishes making it clear who I belong to!" observed the Duc d'Aveyron, amused at his diminutive companion's possessiveness.

Gray dog barked again.

Children in light colors scampered past.

A gardener in navy-blue overalls pruned green shrubs to left.

"We've never run into each other like this, before," observed Rolande, inspecting her red finger nails. "After over a year of we trying to join formally and our plans falling through, we instead end up meeting again by total accident! Who knows, something new, terrific, and big might be in the works!"

"We've never run into each other like this before," reiterated Ferdinande de Godefroy, inspecting proudly her freshly-manicured red nails. "After a year of trying over and over to join up formally and our plans always falling through, we end up meeting by total accident! Who knows, something new, terrific, and big might be in the works!"

The two girls pecked lips, hugged. Both adjusted the angle of other's massive headgear In time, each sister turned to go her separate way.

"I hope we possibly can cross paths again, dear," ventured Rolande in parting.

"I hope we can possibly cross paths again, dear," replied Ferdinande de Godefroy.

"Love you, dear."

"Love you too, dear."

"Bye, bye."

"Bye, bye."

The Two Sisters

IF THIS AFTERNOON'S ENCOUNTER in the Tuilleries Gardens unexpected, still more improbable was it that these girls ever met at all!

While they both the product of same womb, both object of an identical maternal love, Rolande de Montfort and Ferdinande de Godefroy were each long kept unaware her sibling ever existed. As a result, although sisters, the kids were, for all intents and purposes, only the most distant, unacquainted of extended relations.

One girl a redhead, the other a natural blond, each possessing a different surname, and raised in a separate home in separate aristocratic neighborhood. Both were christened in different churches by divergent priests, cared for by same Mama but on alternate weeks. The little dears were permitted traveling only in the family's private jet and motorcade. They never attended school. All their serious social interaction were restricted to mutually exclusive sets of pedigreed playmates and most trusted, primarily female, servants. Celine arranged for her daughters to grow up, as did Britain at the apex of her empire, in *splendid isolation.*

Socially, culturally, if not physically kept far apart, the two girls spent their childhood and early adolescence unaware of the others existence, as if they cloistered nuns, each one belonging to a different meditative *order* on the opposite side of a wide continent.

No less protective of offspring as she was herself fond of winning publicity, this particular mother hen was determined her chicks venture independently outside the nest as seldom as possible until their parent judged them each fully trained to become *Montfort Ladies.*

"Ferdinande and *Missy* are my own creations after all," advised Celine. "They're my own best genes, my own best *DNA!* It's therefore my duty to make sure each darling is secured where she deserves to be—at the top of the social *food chain.*"

In addition, since Rolande de Montfort and Ferdinande de Godefroy were just *half* sisters, "no hopelessly bourgeois reason, no dreadfully middle-class ritual, no blatantly parvenu cause obliged both chicks being raised in same nest." Aside from a biological connection, which in these *sweethearts'* case is but "tenuous," pensive redhead and fashion-setting blonde weren't actually related at all. "It's best keeping them apart," also reasoned their mutual parent. "This way, both my darlings can receive Mama's equal love and care. And besides, what they don't know won't hurt them!"

Money was certainly no obstacle to establishing separate households. Besides, from a real estate standpoint, this made perfect sense. What reason was there for Celine owning all those scattered pieces of property if just one was ever long occupied? If a leak or electrical short circuit developed at one rarely-visited residence, the problem might not be discovered until months later? "Good Lord! That will make a nasty repair bill!" The caretaker of yet another seldom-visited estate, upon concluding *Milady* wasn't returning any time soon, "might move his tramp American girlfriend in, let that dark-roots slut pinch my Sevres porcelain, sell my collection of Claude Lorrain paintings!" The unwatched scoundrel might even accept a bribe, allowing a timber company to level the pretty woods nearby that Celine "loved so much as a little girl?" Also, one summer she might decide spending at a house the exterminator had forgot spraying long ago?

At the mere sight of roaches, the otherwise bold, energetic Mme. de Montfort swift jumped on a chair to scream bloody murder at the top of her lungs. With mice, she "positively lost all control!" And what if "those dreadful furry monsters try taking advantage of me, a weak, helpless female with no big, strong, handsome gentleman to come to my rescue?"

Leaving property vacant too long also invited burglars. Or, in Celine's particular case, offered an opportunity for her empty homes to be ransacked by devoted fans in search of their heroine's priceless relics and mementos. It happened once to the Montfort townhouse in Bordeaux! Raising her chicks in separate nests would solve all of Mama's real estate and vermin worries.

Mama's little dears were *sweethearts* to manage. Neither Rolande de Montfort nor Ferdinande de Godefroy was scared of the *bogeyman*, wet her bed, broke pretty objects, or had tantrums. Neither child put up a fuss when taken to the pediatrician for shots. Resourceful and inventive, each girl could find constructive things to take up her time alone just as easily as when she was in the company of playmates. The two kids never expressed serious loneliness or were long unhappy. They professed no interest in having siblings or were reliant on imaginary friends. They were healthy, always eating their brussels sprouts and drinking their milk, no cavities, *regular*, going to sleep on time, saying all their daily prayers to the Virgin. Both daughters were obedient, respectful of adult authority, pious, deeply affectionate. They were the mirror opposite of brats.

"Giving me so little trouble," said their Mama, "each *sweetheart* deserves a home all her own."

Ultimately, it wasn't real estate upkeep or eccentric theories on child-rearing determining Rolande de Montfort and Ferdinande de Godefroy be kept apart. Each daughter, was for their mama, the living reminder of a far different but no less precious and sadly all-too-brief romantic experience. As such, each child, like the precious individual moment the *little dear* manifested, was in Mama's eyes no less deserving of complete, undistracted veneration. Both daughters possessed a clear right to receive total and undivided love.

For this elaborate juggling act to come anywhere near success however, for a woman to be twice mother of a single child, just a single viable strategy existed. If the plan was extremely difficult pulling off, it wasn't impossible. Especially when considering this woman's—pardon, *lady*'s—unique skill obtaining the assistance of influential gents. In short order, all of Celine's past and present intimates among the masculine powers that be pledged their full cooperation. Even her dapper chums in the media readily guaranteed never divulging the children's existence. In an era when few secrets in high places last more than a month, this particular confidence was maintained for a record longer period of time.

"It would be wonderful if our Celine had a baby!" mused one fan.

"Our Celine deserves children after all she loyally does for us," insisted a second.

"Our Celine's *clock is ticking*!" admonished yet another devoted follower.

If desperate to discover the slightest tidbit of information, to unearth the tiniest piece of gossip about the noted celebrity, the general public never suspected even once that Celine already fulfilled her fans' hope and dream. Still, today, news having finally leaked out, a majority still don't know the truth!

As for the two girls at the center of it all, Rolande de Montfort and Ferdinande de Godefroy didn't learn of their connection until age fifteen. Mama's clockwork—mysterious disappearances every other week and just as regular unexplained returns seven days later; she, teary eyed, out of breath, and laden down like Santa Claus with expensive presents—and Mama's frantic hugs, kisses, pets, placings on lap, requests for her child's forgiveness for mother not devoting every second to "my poor neglected, precious darling" might have aroused suspicion. But with all their meaningful interaction with adults restricted to Mama's gentleman chums and most-trusted female servants (each assigned her own part in the conspiracy) Rolande and Ferdinande possessed no firm reason to think Mama's eccentricities any different from the normal behavior of parents.

At least, the kids never voiced suspicion.

There is reasonable chance the girls came to conclude something peculiar might be afoot. It's conceivable both quite early suspected Mama was hiding from them that she was hopelessly caught up in some sort of adult foolishness, some adult version of one of her children's games. Not wishing to embarrass their doting parent, the girls might have realized how extremely important it was Mama continue believing that her *sweethearts* were unaware of these harmless adult escapades. The girls too perhaps understood it was vital Mama still think she was regarded by her offspring as an all-wise, all-powerful, ever-shielding protector. Her *little darlings* maybe already chose to pretend not noticing Mama's foibles. "After all, what adults don't know can't hurt them."

Whatever the case, the truth at last revealed itself and in a rather amusing manner. An ardent, romantic proposal, penned by a twelve-year-old boy with a crush on one sister, his epistle mentioning Madame de Montfort's name, was accidentally delivered by the postal service to the other sister's door.

Caught thoroughly off guard, Madame de Montfort was at a total loss how to deal with this unforeseen occurrence. When asked by the daughter receiving the misdirected romantic note for whom it was really intended and for what reason Mama's name was included, Celine's panicky, ever vaguer, each time less believable answers only provoked the child to steadily more specific, deeply pointed questions.

At last, Mama burst into refined tears. Falling daintily on knees, she confessed her deception and genteelly begged forgiveness. An elaborate scheme taking many influential adults years to build and perfect came crashing down in just minutes upon being confronted with pubescent longing and blind chance.

Rather than angry or feeling betrayed as the mother hen feared, her chicks were instead much taken with the thought of they being the stimulus for so much grand Italian-opera cloak-and-dagger machinations. Fascinating as it was learning of the existence of a mysterious hidden sibling, still more intriguing for both daughters was it to discover so many noted adults were for years desperate to retain the favor of lowly teenagers, especially girls.

"That's awesome!"

"That's *really* awesome!"

All the same, twelve additional months elapsed before Rolande de Montfort and Ferdinande de Godefroy were actually permitted coming face-to-face.

Each daughter, the perfect embodiment in Mama's eyes of a very separate, quite dissimilar, if no less precious and sadly too brief personal experience, she continued as best she could preserving the girls forever apart, totally unique. Any mutual contact, she dreaded, would result only in lessening the beauty of both, placing into question Mama's equal veneration for each, or at least she wished to believe, equal veneration. Through not revealing to one daughter the whereabouts or showing her photographs of the other, Mama effectively prevented any secret encounters and all mail or telephone communication between the two. She hoped this lack of direct communication would soon make the girls lose further interest in meeting after the initial thrill of unexpected discovery subsided.

Besides living reminders of pleasant memories, her daughters, as Mama was so fond of repeating, "have all my best genes, all my best *DNA*," the time was fast approaching when Rolande de Montfort and Ferdinande de Godefroy must each assume her own proper role in adult society. Soon, both teenagers must join Mama, Auntie Philippine, Auntie Léonie, their cousins, as previously too did Grandmother Marie and Great-Auntie Bernarde, as one of the world's grandest of all grand courtesans. Celine, was in fact, already launched on a survey to determine which of her many distinguished gentlemen chums was best suited belonging to each of her charming, talented daughters. Until recently, everything appeared proceeding as smooth on the path to fulfillment as in every generation for more than 550 years of *Montfort ladies*. No unpredictable last-minute snag should be allowed to block a correct and natural process.

Still, twelve additional months denying them contact increased rather than diminished the girls' mutual curiosity, Celine reluctantly agreed to a compromise. Doing so while she yet held the upper hand. "Yes, periodic encounters can occur," Celine told them separately. "Although these meetings must take place only when and where Mama chooses and according to Mama's nonnegotiable terms." Later on, after each daughter was "securely placed in a powerful gentleman's bed, she provided that powerful gentleman's arm to loyally clutch, his magisterial shoulder to rub with submissive cheek," the two girl "could go chattering away to their tender hearts' content." That's if by that time, Rolande de Montfort and Ferdinande Godefroy "weren't so preoccupied being politically influential mistresses, thought of private sisterly meetings ever crossed their lovely minds." In the meantime, so long as the two chicks continued living under roofs Mama owned, remained entirely dependent on Mama paying the bills, Mama possessed the unquestioned authority and right to set the rules.

"You're both my creations after all," Celine reminded them. "I made you two! You're therefore also my responsibility!"

The two sisters met several times during the following eighteen months. Their visits, alternating between the *Baroque* townhouse where Ferdinande de Godefroy lived on the Right Bank in Paris, and the one at which Rolande de Montfort lived on, Left. The girls came together on birthdays, Easter Sundays, and on Christmas Eve. Dressed in their finest, their hair all dolled-up, they found these long-fought-for and against-all-odds-attained reunions tremendous fun.

Before placing her daughters side by side at the table for formal dinners, Celine insisted taking them first with her to Mass. Admittedly, the two girls did much to distract the rest of the congregation with their perpetual giggles, bursts of suppressed laughter, physical gesticulations, and teenage off-color jokes. No need worrying about sibling rivalry! If connected by blood, growing up completely apart in mutual ignorance made the two regard each other as best girlfriends rather than competing sisters.

Once her chicks were back at the beautiful, sweeping, antique dinner table situated in salon with vaulted ceiling and walls decorated with Tiepolo frescoes, Celine employed these closely choreographed encounters as opportunities enabling her most titled, wealthy, elite, and picky clientele to take relaxed, extended inspections.

"No, no. Not just yet, my favorite gentleman," Celine would indicate without need for words. "My chicks aren't yet quite old enough. They still require another year or so to fully blossom. But fear not, my most privileged chums. Next year or so, you'll be given first choice. Remember, my chums, *patience is a virtue.*"

Any moment her girls threatened raising a subject that might make them appear for the gentlemen present as too cerebral, Celine immediately shifted the conversation. Under Celine's delicate, subtle, but firm direction, Rolande de Montfort and Ferdinande de Godefroy launched into hours upon hours of giggling, animated *girl talk.* They related the latest celebrity gossip, debated the newest hair style, discussed their newest set of heels and sheerest pantyhose. The two ruminated on the color pink, exchanged tips on management of their equally splendid legs, confided the right means of better displaying their equally fine busts. The sisters offered one another personal judgments on various perfumes, eyeliners, and lipstick.

Whenever Celine abruptly announced the current visit over—"The best time to part is precisely when you feel most like staying," Mama always believed—the sisters exchanged heartfelt hugs, warm kisses, endearing pets, rocked back and forth together gently, pair lovingly united as a single girlish being. They expressed earnest teary-eyed pledges to link up again alone soon. Both were also fully resigned to accept that, under present conditions, pledges, no matter how sincere and genuine, could never be more than *pledges*. After one particularly fond meeting, the girls surreptitiously scribbled down and exchanged telephone numbers and mailing addresses—independent links of communication that Celine promptly filched. Such tremendous innocent, uncomplicated fun the sisters enjoyed when together, even despite Mama's constant interference. Rolande de Montfort and Ferdinande de Godefroy both loved, each shielded at her heart, these priceless memories for the rest of her gilded cage life.

Repeatedly, as the date boldly marked down on separate calendars in bright-red ink indicating next mutual encounter neared, the sisters could rarely sleep. They often broke out into violent shivers, made themselves ill, needed to be put to bed, frequently erupted into furious sobs. So great was their mutual anticipation, collective longing for a day and hour, which the closer it actually came, seemed so tortuously farther away.

Yet for all the pure, unforgettable happiness these meetings brought to each sister, despite all the frequent, perfectly sincere declarations both made that their encounters should continue forever, visiting still came to an end. The passionate, highly emotional, overheated, possessive camaraderie of naïve teenage girls wasn't permitted space or freedom to expand into a wider, more complex adult bond. The mutually fulfilling, soul mate affinity needed for preserving attachments beyond initial thrill of discovery was denied opportunity taking root.

Except, that is, on one occasion.

Precious Moments

"COME! COME WITH ME, Ferdinande! Let me show you something I've got!"

"Oh yes, Rolande, show me, please!"

One of the sisters' final encounters occurred during a thought-provoking autumn afternoon—at a birthday party, to be precise—held at the townhouse where Celine's younger daughter lived in the 7th Arrondissement, on the Right Bank of Paris. The tall chestnut and plain trees situated just beyond the polished oak-framed front French windows were now become a carnival of splendid natural colors: red, orange, blue, green, yellow, purple. Never previous too had a brilliant tangerine sun so well commanded a cobalt-blue cloudless sky as the glowing orb retreated queenly beneath a far distant line of light-brown sandstone medieval battlements.

"Let's go, Ferdinande. Quick before Mama is back!"

"Yes, Rolande, before Mama gets back."

The lady of the house abruptly summoned elsewhere on urgent domestic business, Celine's "best genes, best *DNA*" wasted no time in seizing the unexpected chance to speed off on their own. One sister enthusiastically took the others hand and rushed them both upstairs so that elder girl might be introduced to younger's constantly growing, ever-burgeoning library. One containing an increasingly impressive number of first-edition out-of-print books; famous handwritten correspondence; unpublished manuscripts; rare daguerreotypes; bound periodicals; old maps charts, lists, and diagrams. It was a collection providing readers priceless insight into every conceivable *—ism, —ian, neo—, pre—, —esque, —ite, —ist, pro—, anti—, semi* and *post—* existing or thought existing during the last five thousand years of human history.

"Awesome! It's awesome, Rolande, dear! It's awesome!"

"Thank you, Ferdinande, dear. I'm—*awesome* pleased you think so."

"It's awesome!"

"Go and take a closer look, dear."

"I certainly will, dear."

Ferdinande de Godefroy, who possesses infinitely more intellectual heavy artillery, far greater cerebral bomb load capacity than anyone, least of all she believes, was transfixed by what was now before her.

Large and small; new and old; fine condition and dog-eared; weighty, light; narrow, wide; colorful and plain; illustrated, unillustrated; written in multiple languages at numerous times by different authors both male and female living in scattered places and in dissimilar historic eras books, collected correspondence, and bound periodicals totally covered three of the large double room's papered four walls. Save for shelf levels, the literary, scholarly works occupied almost every inch of the area from hardwood oak floor to high- vaulted ceiling.

For a visitor only four foot ten inches tall, even with benefit of heels, the spectacle before her green eyes appeared yet even grander, more imposing, still.

"Awesome!" exclaimed Ferdinande de Godefroy. "*Really* awesome! I wish I could explain, say exactly how I feel right this second, tell what seeing all this makes me feel. But today you'll need to be satisfied with me saying your books are awesome, *really* awesome, Rolande, dear."

Several minutes elapsed as Ferdinande de Godefroy meditated deep on the library from wall to wall to wall. She pondered the magnificent tomes top to bottom, then from left to right, right to left. She inspected them first slow, then fast. Up, then down. Doing so once, twice, three, four, five, six times.

"Awesome!"

She then began excitedly reading aloud the names of the authors.

"Simone Weil, Marx, Aristotle, Hegel, Dante, Turgenev, Shaw, St. John of the Cross, Hardy, Mann, Lucretius, Shakespeare, Racine, Sister Juana Ines de la Cruz, Jane Austen, Rilke, George Eliot, Heidegger,

Spenser, Rabelais, Montesquieu, Boswell, Duns Scotus, Darwin, Feuerbach, Goethe, Hobbes, Josephus, Machiavelli, Plato, Huysman, Dostoyevsky, Chaucer, Plotinus, Abelard, Heine, Apollinaire, Pushkin, Locke, Schiller…Wow!" She at last finished reciting these names.

The fascinated miniature onlooker now turned to the writers found on other shelves. Once more, she recited in an upbeat, dainty, girlish voice, "Spinoza, Moliere, Addison, Steele, Xenophon, Tacitus, Russell, Rumi, Pope, Akhmatova, Berdyaev, Mommsen, Balzac, Thackeray, Lamb, Arendt, Petrarca, Sappho, Husserl, Cervantes, St. Teresa of Avila, Tolstoy, Foucault, Blake, Spengler, Joyce, Roger Bacon, Wieland, Pascal, Kant, Tsvetaeva, Ricardo, Venerable Bede, Froissart, Arthur Young, John of Salisbury, Croce, Yeats, Hazlitt, Biruni, Rousseau, Dickinson, Proust…"

On and still further on, Ferdinande de Godefroy eagerly recited, "Kierkegaard, Strindberg, Leibniz, Montaigne, Lessing, *Romance of the Rose*, Quinet, Ariosto, Schopenhauer, Lefebvre, Tasso, Yeats, Visari, Ficte, *Autobiography of Edith Stein*, Albertus Magnus, Ibsen, Lefebvre, William James, Bentham, Taine, Matthew Paris, Erasmus, *The Cathars*, Mechtild of Magdeburg, William of Newburgh, *St. Bernard of Clairvaux*, John of Wallingford, John of Fordun, Braudel, Foner, Popper…"

The young viewer speculated, gasping, "How many tomes are there here, all together?" She at last halted for breath. "Lord knows! Surely, there are thousands. No, obviously, there are thousands! Yes, surely, thousands! Awesome! No, *really* awesome!"

Like a prima ballerina, Ferdinande de Godefroy instinctively performed a graceful and absolutely perfect pirouette atop the darkwood floor with outstretched left foot.

"Take as much time as you want and need, dear!" urged Rolande in choked voice, much touched by sister's reaction, greatly moved by new friend's appraisal of her most fond, precious possessions. "I like collecting books, as you see, Ferdinande dear, especially, ones on history, art, philosophy, and literature. You're the first girl I've shown my collection to."

"Ooh, mi!"

"In fact, dear, you're, the only person besides Mama and the servants who knows my collection even exists! Mama's gentleman caller dandies like stupid Prince Markovsky wouldn't at all be pleased if they learned *young sweet things* read this sort of scholarly, highbrow material. In fact, Ferdinande dear, you're the only one outside No. 3 Rue Artemis, the only one else in the whole wide world, who knows my collection exists!"

"Ooh, goodness gracious!"

"That's why I brought you to see it!" illuminated curator Rolande, fiddling with a white bow in her fiery red locks. Blessed, grateful tears came to her deep, watery, pensive gray-green feminine eyes. "It was so important to me you come and look at my book and old map and chart collection—even more important still, that you've got the precise same opinion about the collection as me! Learning of my collection, Mama decided to call it the *Missy Collection.* Accumulating the collection also makes me feel so really awesome inside." Rolande broke off, her words become unsure. Seconds later, she resumed at unsteady cadence. "It's hard to explain precisely what that kind of splendid, exciting feeling inside is all about...yet...but...well, you get the idea I'm sure, dear."

"Yes, don't worry, dear. I know what that kind of awesome feeling inside is," responded Ferdinande de Godefroy, also gratefully teary eyed, cadence of her words unsteady. Long, thick cherry-blond hair obscured her attractive adolescent face. "I'm also so, so...*honored.* I feel exactly the same kind of *awesome* inside, dear, because you want so much for me to see your *Missy Collection,* your *Missy Archive.*" After a reflective pause, Ferdinande de Godefroy confessed, "I'm especially so, so, so honored, dear...I'm most of all honored...because you believe there's value to my personal opinion. No one else ever thinks my opinion is worth anything! No one else cares what I've got to say!"

She explained, "No one speaks ill of me directly to my face. Still, not a day seems to pass when I don't hear not so inaudible phrases, catch not-so-distant whispers just behind my back like: *'Oh, never mind what she's babbling. That's just silly, little Ferdinande'* or *'Oh, don't bother paying attention to little Ferdinande. She always means well, it's true. Unfortunately, she's doomed to be nothing but a fashion*

81

plate, just a pretty face' or *'Oh, here chatterbox little Ferdinande goes again babbling nonsense! She's certainly cute all right but sadly, that's all she's got going for her!'* or *'Why doesn't little Ferdinande leave us alone and go upstairs and look at herself in the mirror'* or *'If only the poor child had been given just an ounce of brains! Yet I guess all God's children can't be so lucky.'"*

Ferdinande confided, "I heard similar comments his morning too, Rolande." Then smiling teary eyed at her more erudite sister, she revealed, appreciative, "You're the first person in ever so long to believe what I say is worth hearing."

"That's terrible, dear, that's terrible!" exclaimed Rolande angrily, stomping her right foot, wielding girlish left fist in emphasis. "That's terrible, terrible! It's horrendous!"

Missy stroked her unhappy sister's long, thick cherry-blond hair in sympathy. She gave a comradely peck to her so misunderstood friend's unblemished forehead. "That's horrible! If I'd been told earlier about this, I'd have gone and punched—"

"No, no! I don't want you to be upset on my account, dear!" pleaded Ferdinande de Godefroy resignedly. "In fact, I'm starting to become used to it. It must be kinda like the way doctors say they learn to stop thinking about seeing naked bodies and morticians claim handling corpses becomes just a job. What do American office seekers call it? I'm developing 'a *thick skin.*'"

"All the same, dear, that's a terrible way they talked to you!" again insisted Rolande earnestly from beneath long, thick, fiery red hair obscuring pretty face. "That's no proper way to speak of about you! There's no reason you need start developing a *thick skin.* Your opinion is of great value. I find great value to your opinion, Ferdinande, great value in your point of view! And don't let anyone convince you otherwise! If that's how others think about, my dear, it only goes to further prove their own opinions aren't worth anything! From the moment we first met, I could see you're really smart—"

"I'm not so sure about that last bit, dear, but thanks anyway."

"No, dear!" admonished Rolande. Her earlier choked voice grew strong, confident, and steady as she took her weeping friend's right hand delicately but firm in both own. "Now, no more of such foolishness do you hear, Ferdinande, dear! Don't talk nonsense like that! From this day forth, I don't want to hear any such foolishness out of you again! Hear! Hear! I won't permit one single more peep of this 'I'm not sure about that last bit, but thanks anyway' foolishness. Do you hear me? Hear!"

Ferdinande de Godefroy smiled and nodded, humble. As if a prima ballerina, she drew a second swift, graceful, and absolutely perfect circle in the darkwood floor with outstretched left foot. Grateful tears welled up in her so feminine green eyes.

"I don't care what others say, dear," continued Rolande shieldingly, providing her unhappy companion a handkerchief. "I know you're really smart! You're really brainy! So for me getting the approval of a really smart, really brainy person like you isn't just nice. It's as you say, an honor! It's a big honor!" Rolande adjusted her short skirt.

"Have you read them all, dear?" asked Ferdinande de Godefroy, wiping her teary, so feminine green eyes with proffered handkerchief. Earlier sniffles remained detectable in her melodic ladylike voice. She adjusted own short skirt while again contemplating the impressive bookshelves. "Have you read every last one of these, marvelous, too-many-to-ever-count books, dear?"

"No, not all, dear," confessed *Missy*. "But I'm certainly going to try."

"Don't worry, dear. I know you'll read them all too!" assured Ferdinande de Godefroy. "Well, no, I bet you don't read and investigate them all!" A smile arose on her face, one as sly, artfully confiding as was her melodic voice. She waxed, poetic, "No, Rolande, dear, you won't be able to ever read them all since more books and volumes and old maps and charts and quarterlies and periodicals and scholarly tomes keep coming like water over Victoria Falls or waves from the mouth of the St. Lawrence! As soon as it appears, all's been done, yet still more books and journals and documents and collections of correspondence and old maps showing griffins, monsters, and men with faces in their chest living in Africa at the equator arrive in the mail to take the mountain of 'just finished old ones' place!" She hugged Rolande tight and pecked her learned sister's forehead affectionately. "That's not the worst problem in the world to be unable to surmount, it seems to me. Is it? In fact, I like it better, dear if you're never able to read all those splendid books—yes, indeed, I prefer it that way!"

"To tell you the truth, my Ferdinande dearest," replied the redhead librarian Ferdinande now held in loving arms. "I prefer it that way too!"

The pair giggled.

Releasing her best, most intimate friend at last, Ferdinande de Godefroy, like a prima ballerina, performed yet a third swift, graceful pirouette atop the darkwood floor.

"You'll find more than a few times, dear," counseled Missy, "that the most really awesome books with some of the most really awesome *stuff* to read and investigate are the work of authors you've never previously heard of!"

"Ooh! Is that so, dear?"

"Yes, dear, it's so! Makes you always keep reevaluating the world, doesn't it?"

"I'm positive you know a whole lot more than any girl who's gone to school, dear!" guaranteed Ferdinande de Godefroy. "I'm positive you know a whole lot more than all the girls who go to school…combined! And then a lot more than that besides!"

The cherry blonde further walked about the double room pensively, her arms energetically akimbo. Again, she read off the names of still more authors whose famous writings were here to be seen, to be picked up and read.

"Buber, Manzoni, Weber, Macaulay, Carlyle, Diderot, Boaz, *Diary of St. Simon*, Chekhov, Virgil, *Der Niebelungenlied*, Grotius, Catullus, Moses Mendelssohn, Voltaire, Boethius, Aeschylus, Philo of Alexandria, Schelling, Aulard, Donne, Berkeley, *Pepys Diary*, Helvetius, Fromm, Brentano, Toynbee, Strabo, T. S. Eliot, Joinville, Cowper, Al-Maqrizi, Fielding, Horace, Musil, *Collected Letters of John and Abigail Adams*, Chateaubriand, Grotius, Robert Browning, Aristophanes, Mickiewicz, Cicero, Seneca…"

Her inspection of the books at last complete, Ferdinande de Godefroy now looked up at the shelves near the vaulted Tiepolo fresco ceiling. These shelves, her own tiny stature made appear even more distant. These uppermost levels were stacked to bursting with old bound issues of the *Revue des Deux Mondes, Cahiers du Sud, Deutschen Literatur, Blackwood's Edinburgh Magazine, American Historical Review* along with old bound copies of scholarly presentations delivered at the French Academy, at the British Royal Academy, and at Paris, Heidelberg, and Gottingen universities.

"Did you read those famous journals and periodicals and speeches found way, way up at the top too, dear?"

"Yes, dear," answered Rolande with just pride. "Yes, I've read those way, way up at the top too!"

"Awesome!"

"I don't climb the ladder unless Mama is safely busy downstairs. I'm actually forbidden to be on the ladder at all. Mama claims seeing me climb the ladder gives her apoplexy.'"

Rolande mimicked Celine, parodying their mother's often employed *feather-brains* voice and *dimwit blond* physical comportment.

"Mama says, 'Seeing my baby scale the dangerous heights causes a *fragile female* like her mother to instantly lose whatever little wits she does have!'"

The two sisters exploded into protracted, furious giggles.

When the duo were at last exhausted from collective merriment, recovered their mutual breath, long, thick cherry-blond and fiery red hair still covered the two's pretty faces.

"Poor Mama!" her progeny said fondly. "How does she ever manage!"

Rolande de Montfort and Ferdinande de Godefroy again mimicked Celine in both voice and body.

"How does Mama ever manage! Life is so difficult for a *fragile female*."

"Have you any favorite subject, dear?" inquired Ferdinande de Godefroy at last.

"The Middle Ages."

"What an exciting time that was, Rolande, dear."

"I first became interested in the Middle Ages as a little girl while watching a television show on modern farming. The narrator talked about the contrast between farmers today and farmers in the Middle Ages. It caught my heart, and so I began some reading. I haven't stopped since. Then, of course, there's my own literary name."

"*The Song of Roland* (e)!"

"Yes, how could I ever forget, *The Song of Roland(e)*"

"I love *the Middle Ages* too, dear. I love *The Middle Ages* too!" cried Ferdinande de Godefroy. She keenly recognized a soul mate, delighted discovering not just a sister but a fellow spirit. "Those first few centuries after the fall of Rome were certainly benighted, scramble for cover, ignorant, rough and tumble. But the entire period wasn't anywhere near as *dark* as most people think! King Arthur! Tristan and Iseult! Averroes! Saladin! Maimonides! Ibn Khaldun! St. Francis! Giotto! Abelard and Heloise! Chivalry! Marie de France! Cimabue! Fra Angelico! Petrarca!"

"Tragic sagas and courtly love!"

"Don't forget brave knights and fair ladies! Troubadours, princesses rescued from castles! *Romanesque* and *Gothic* cathedrals, stained glass! Jousting, illuminated manuscripts!"

"Eleanor of Aquitaine, dear."

"Yes, dear," seconded Ferdinande de Godefroy. "Eleanor of Aquitaine! She was a *really* awesome lady! She was smarter than most of the men of her day! It truly must be so, that Eleanor of Aquitaine was stunningly beautiful. Not only did her allies say she was stunningly beautiful but also her worst enemies and most bitter detractors! Enemies, detractors who might naturally be expected to say she looked like a Medusa!"

"Don't forget Jeanne d'Arc lived in the Middle Ages."

"Yes, and also did Blanche of Castile, Margaret of Anjou, Isabelle the She-Wolf, St. Hildegard of Bingen, St. Catherine of Siena!"

"I'd like to write about the Middle Ages too, dear," revealed Rolande.

"Well, with all your ever-wider reading and your brainy head, I'm sure you'll succeed, dear! Become a true expert!"

"I want to write *stuff* that's really significant about the Middle Ages," elaborated the scholarly redhead. "I want to write *stuff* that will make all my reading and investigating worthwhile. I want to be the author of books and articles that are one day found in all the world's big libraries and learned institutions! I want to be an author of *stuff* that the most celebrated professors and greatest academics assign their students to read and ask their students questions about in class!"

She mused, "They'll ask, *'What did Rolande de Montfort write about X? What does Rolande de Montfort teach the world about Y? Have you carefully studied what Rolande de Montfort discovered about Z?'* I want students to need to cram all night in order to pass their tough *Rolande de Montfort Examinations,* to be awarded their *Rolande de Montfort Degree, Rolande de Montfort Prize*! I want, Ferdinande dear, it to be so that one day people who go to school tell their famous chums with lots of Latin initials after names, *'If you want to learn a lot of truly awesome 'stuff,' want to learn a lot of really terrific 'stuff' about the Middle Ages you simply, simply, simply must, must, must read what Rolande de Montfort wrote! Rolande de Montfort might not be educated, she might never have gone to school, but that doesn't matter. Eleanor of Aquitaine, Blanche of Castile weren't educated, never went to school either! You simply, simply, simply, have got, got, got to read what Rolande de Montfort says about the Middle Ages! Unless you read the 'stuff' she wrote about that part of history, you'll never, never, never truly understand the Middle Ages!'"*

Rolande stopped at last, out of breath, heart pounding, lungs exhausted. She leaned on her soul mate's right shoulder for support.

"Ooh, wee! Sometimes, hen, I discuss the Middle Ages I just can't control myself! I turn into what Mama calls a *fragile female*!"

"Well, don't worry! I'm sure you'll succeed, Rolande dear!" promised Ferdinande de Godefroy with all teenage earnestness. She gave a reassuring peck to her fellow spirit's unblemished forehead. She loyally smoothed *Missy*'s fiery red locks now gone every which way. "Wait, I mean, I mean I *know* you will write really important, awesomely significant, path-breaking *stuff*! You can depend on it, dear! The *stuff* on the Middle Ages you're going to write is going to get into all the big libraries. It is going to be assigned to students; asked questions about in class, lectures, seminars; even made into movies!"

Ferdinande continued, "What you write about the Middle Ages, Rolande dear, is going to be admired by all the people who go to school, all those with all those Latin initials after their names. You can depend on it!"

Miniature cherry blonde paused. A twinkle was now in this little lady's so feminine green eyes, a broad smile upon her moist, red-painted lips.

"You'll write great *stuff* like that, Rolande!" her sister predicted. "You'll be famous and respected all around the world! I'll be able to brag to everyone, *'Ferdinande was present when it all began! Ferdinande saw it all happen with her own eyes!'* That's no different really from people who said, *'I was at the storming of the Bastille! I saw it actually happen! I was there and saw it all unfold!'* In fact, I'll be able to say, *'Ferdinande was there even before it all began! Ferdinande knew it was all going to happen—before anyone else did or even imagined it could happen!'*"

The prima ballerina executed a fourth graceful pirouette atop the hard wood floor.

"Bless you, dear!" responded Missy, immensely moved.

"Say, dear," queried Ferdinande de Godefroy, "have you started writing?"

"Actually, yes, dear!" answered Rolande. "But please understand I'm just at the very, very beginning! So far I've only made notes, lists, and scratchings so far. I've not even told Mama about it. You're the first person in the whole world I've ever told, dear. Please promise not to tell Mama. I don't want my Middle Ages project to be learned about by anyone but you until I've really gotten started."

"I promise, dear!" pledged Ferdinande de Godefroy, again with all teenage girl earnestness. "I promise, dear! I won't tell anyone on earth until you give me permission."

"Bless you, my dear!"

"And bless you too, my dear!"

Girls pecked red-painted lips, pressed hands.

"Say, dear?" ventured Ferdinande de Godefroy after a moment. "I wouldn't even presume telling you what and when and how to write… but gathering all that information; all that profound *stuff*; all those many brainy facts and figures, details, and statistics together before you start…collecting all that *stuff* by yourself will be terribly time-consuming. Maybe, if I absolutely and swearing on the Bible declare I won't interfere a single time with your authorship, I could…I could do…"

"Do research for me, my Ferdinande dear?"

"Yes, my Rolande dear! I can be your research assistant! Sometimes if you're busy with important writing in one town and still need more *stuff* looked up in another, you could send me to find it? You can say to me, 'Ferdinande, dear, I need more *stuff* about A. I also need a picture of B. I need to take a look at C, be positively sure D is E and not F. Could you go and find it?'"

"Of course, my dear," replied Rolande. "Of course! You come and help me! It'll be even more fun and stimulating that way, we doing it as a twosome! We'll do this significant stuff as a…duo! We'll be…the *Middle Ages Duo*!"

"Awesome, my dear. I can't wait to get started!"

"Awesome, my Ferdinande, dear. I can't wait to get started!"

The two girls pecked each other's red-painted lips.

Pecked again.

Hugged one another tight.

Then tighter, more loving still.

Humming a mutually favorite melancholy, faraway song, two separate questing souls merged into a single spiritual, unmeddled-with feminine being.

Time passed.

Minutes elapsed.

"We'll show the world!" the girls now said as one. "We don't need silly education to be famous scholars or great academics. We don't need to go to school in order to find or do important *stuff*!"

"Praise the Virgin! So here, my two precious darlings are at last found, hidden away!" exclaimed Celine as if she an amateur actress bursting upon the stage at the key moment of the critical scene in a summer camp rendering of a famous play. She waved her sculpted arms high in the air, let jewelry around her slender neck go all askew. Long cherry-blond hair covered lovely face. All these rehearsed overdrawn gesticulations were calculated to add further melodramatic effect.

"All praise to the Virgin! Mama's located you two at last! *A woman's work is never done*! No sooner is Mama required downstairs to mediate a silly, foolish argument between the cook and the delivery man, than her two lovely creations go speeding away on their own without telling where they're off to! You practically gave your mama *apoplexy*, sent your mama six feet under!"

After first casting a long, reflective glance at the volumes covering three of the double room's four walls from hardwood oak floor to vaulted, Tiepolo-fresco, molded ceiling, Madame de Montfort then confided in her soft, melodic natural voice, "Though, of course, this is exactly where Mama should've known first to look! How again so *scatterbrain female* your parent is!"

"Ferdinande and I are discussing the Middle Ages," informed Rolande, a large book containing photographs of stained glass windows in both her hands, just taken from one crowded shelf. "Both of us find the Middle Ages such an awesome subject, Mama. It's a topic ever so much fun to discuss and study!"

"Yes, we're going to be *the Middle Ages Duo*, Mama!" announced the other member of this learned dainty pair. "Rolande and I are embarking on some significant *stuff* that's going to one day be found in all the big libraries and universities. *Stuff* that will always be mentioned, praised by all the people with lots of Latin initials after their names! That sounds awesome fun, doesn't it, Mama? Rolande wants me to be her research assistant, to travel around, and to gather information for her when she's too busy where she is to go by herself. Sounds awesome fun! We're going to be *the Middle Ages Duo*! Isn't that great, Mama, so exciting?"

"Well, the Middle Ages, *Middle Ages Duos,* and awesome *stuff* can wait till later, my girls!" proclaimed Celine, tone of her voice leaving the two kids in no doubt the speaker's words must be at once obeyed.

Celine angrily snatched the book of stained glass photographs from Rolande's hands and placed it back on a random bookshelf. Next, she delivered Ferdinande de Godefroy an almost physically painful glare of maternal disapproval, one leaving her in no doubt that any further attempt trespassing on the forbidden intellectual domain would bring the girl the severest punishment.

"Mama," she told both children, "promises her two creations can still embark for valiant 'days of yore.' Mama promises her darlings can still become fair princesses rescued from castles by handsome heroes on white steeds later! Later! But in the meantime, first things first!"

Applying each daughter a firm smack on her little fanny, Celine hustled the pretty medievalists toward a door leading to stairway. "Come along, come along! Let Mama straighten your frocks! Let Mama straighten your panties! Get the hair out of your cute faces! Don't stoop, stand erect! Be the proper young ladies Mama spent so much time and energy training you to be! We've got distinguished guests in the parlor! Important gentlemen wish to see you both!"

If each sister's knowledge of the other's existence achieved only through blind chance, so too was it that Rolande de Montfort and Ferdinande de Godefroy were ever permitted engaging in serious, intimate, meaningful conversation. Only pure luck enabled them to abandon heavily choreographed upper-class *chitchat* and speak intimately as trusted, devoted comrades. It proved an encounter enabling them to discover the two actually shared a bond potentially far more enduring, mutually fulfilling than sheer accidental tie of blood. Unfortunately, a second such opportunity to escape Celine's watchful eyes and sensitive ears never arose.

During the remainder of the supervised visits, all discussion was restricted to formalized banter at the dinner party table or upon exiting Mass. All occurring under Celine's polite, refined but iron unquestioned supervision.

At the close of eighteen months, with every subject for patrician *small talk* covered, little was left to ruminate upon but the weather. The sisters' dialogue, once so lively, now sagged. Repeatedly they shifted inelegantly in cherrywood red damask chairs. First once, then twice, a third time. Shoes tapped nervously. Anxious fingers drummed preoccupied on ebony tables. Forced coughs began to be heard; less-than-genteel observations voiced. Pairs of pretty young legs no longer crossed. Each sister, coming to believe she had rashly disclosed her deepest, most intimate, private teenage secrets to someone proving but a chance acquaintance, Rolande de Montfort and Ferdinande de Godefroy both felt stupid, ashamed, embarrassed. Each became steadily more uneasy and suspicious in the other's presence. After an unexpected heavy rain prevented the next visit, neither girl asked Celine to reschedule it.

An additional twelve months later, just as predicted, with Rolande de Montfort and Ferdinande de Godefroy each now sharing the bed of a powerful gentleman, their calendar filled with many new social commitments, little time was left to consider further sisterly encounters. As Mama wished it so, the living reminders of two different precious and all-too-short personal experiences were to live forever apart.

You Better Ask the Lady First

TIME PASSED.

Months succeeding.

Seasons change.

The ancient oak and plain and chestnut trees in the garden running parallel the right embankment first clothed in fullest, beckoning, majestic green, were later dressed in no less memorable and dynamic shades of orange, gold, sandstone, and red. When this performance too, so splendid to a stroller's eye at last was done, the tree mantels dropped exhausted, wizened on dark-brown or battleship-gray dirt and gravel. For long months, the famous enclosure was left empty, cold, bare, and, to an observer's eye, lonely and abandoned. Happily, fresh buds appearing on the branches in recent weeks announced nature's cycle was beginning anew. Soon, these winding, pensive walkways once more would receive a coat of many colors. Within those historic grounds, near a *neoclassical* fountain again jetting white foam after shutdown over the winter, children, earlier seen bundled up in prams, now toddled forth on their brave, adventurous own power.

As time passes, so also human events.

Countess de Montfort made her next celebrated, much-anticipated, sold-out, scalpers-nirvana, appearance at the Garnier Opera. In frantic expectation of her arrival, much of central Paris was jammed for hours beforehand. The lady's superb performances of the piano concertos of Beethoven in E-Flat Major, Mendelssohn in G-Minor, Schumann in A, Brahms in D-Minor, Grieg in A-Minor and Shostakovich in C, were available within the week on *CD* as mobs of fans rushed with bated breath to *Amazon*, department stores, and music shops so they might each obtain their own priceless, irreplaceable copy. For those unable finding one, pirated versions were soon available made in China, Singapore, Thailand, and Vietnam.

Questioned when she was to launch her next international tour, Celine announced the worldwide concert circuit scheduled to travel throughout Europe, North and South America, the Far East would commence soon after the upcoming French parliamentary *general election.*

I

Ten days later, France returned to the polls. Voter participation was massive. Almost 90 percent of those registered took the opportunity expressing a personal judgment on their nation's leadership. By and large, it was a negative one. If the assassination of *Little Marie* stymied the collective forces of liberal social reform, her tragic passing by no means eliminated the immense discontent for which the young refugee artist and her thought-provoking frescoes gave so inspiring a voice. While the conservatives initially profited from the confusion provoked by the magical teenager's death, it wasn't long before the reasons making the status quo, so deeply unpopular, reemerged. The long governing right-of-center bloc lost nearly 250 seats in the National Chamber of Deputies. Many of these defeats occurred in historically *safe* party machine strongholds. Even the prime minister and four other cabinet officers (the ministers of Foreign Affairs, Interior, Health, and Justice) abruptly found themselves unemployed.

If still managing to preserve a single-vote majority and limping continuance in office, the once invincible conservative bloc now looked fatally weakened, mortally reduced in domestic legislative power and ability to project global influence. According to both reliable outside observers and many of its own surviving members, the government would fall in just a matter of weeks. Their once canyon-width margin for maneuver in the National Chamber of Deputies evaporated. Coalition leaders, so predicted respected commentators, would abandon any attempt at passing controversial legislation until following the next presidential race.

Unfortunately, this dramatic reversal proved far less significant or lasting than expected. As before, in the absence of *Little Marie* as unifying symbol and with her original band of disciples, *The Five Good Ladies*, pushed aside by gate crashing, eleventh-hour enthusiasts, the vast but heterogeneous opposition rapidly forfeited its new dynamism. Promising voters to inaugurate an unprecedented age of freedom, justice, and opportunity for all, opposition forces soon collapsed into bitter disputes over how, where, when and above all *who* was to enact their martyred heroine's reforms. Despite its ever-increasing unpopularity, the long-reigning conservative coalition soon appeared likely to remain ensconced in power for the foreseeable future.

Not all were disappointed.

Three days after the result of the *general election* was announced, President Thomas Belanger selected Finance Minister Alexander Markovsky, a survivor of their bloc's near-fatal rout, to form the next government. With all his party rivals defeated at the polls, Belanger not permitted a third term, and the opposition fallen back into its normal infighting, Markovsky was assured, save for improbable developments, becoming in just nine months the next president of France.

II

The family of Celine de Montfort's Thursday-evening gentleman caller were now journeyed far since they escaped the Bolsheviks with little more than shirt on back or skirt around waist. The Markovsky clan were now traveled many miles from the days when these erstwhile cronies of Peter and Catherine the Great, these former obscenely wealthy princes and princesses, once barely eked by in Montmartre exile through playing the fiddle in *Metro* stations or accordion on street with performing monkey, telling fortunes at village fairs, serving as maids to fat tyrannical bourgeois housewives, or by giving deportment lessons to gawky daughters of *nouveau riche* social climber industrialists.

"I praise, I bless, I honor you from the bottom of my heart, Your Grace!" expressed Celine dutifully from across the secure telephone line she possessed at No. 3 Rue Artemis to among other dapper gents: Prince Markovsky. "Now that we have such a brilliant, skilled, and, above all, Christian, God-fearing leader, I've not the slightest doubt France will at last achieve her rightful position as inspiration to the entire world!"

"That's so very kind of you, *sweetheart*," replied her illustrious chum, deeply flattered. "I'll to do my best."

"No need for worry, Your Grace! Success for my wise, handsome lord and master, splendid achievement for my personal champion, my very own defender, protector is assured. A *woman's intuition* never fails!"

"Thank you for placing such confidence in me, *sweetheart.*"

"Since my prince—*my prince charming*—is in short time to become president of our republic, it might not any longer be proper I keep addressing him as *Your Grace*, Your Grace?"

"Perhaps not," conceded Prince Markovsky, speculating on all the path-breaking historic plans he now intended setting in motion. "However, because my *sweetheart* is both a monarchist—"

"Long live the king!" Celine giggled.

"Because my *sweetheart* is both a monarchist and a monarchist so devoted to me, I thereby grant the dear permission to keep addressing me as she wishes."

"May the Virgin preserve you!"

"I'm touched."

"I hope His Grace won't allow his new august responsibilities to keep him from still visiting his loyal protégée on Thursday evenings? My charming, brave hero knows how so very much his *little woman* looks forward to our weekly private get-togethers. My prince understands how his faithful *little woman* instantly bursts into tears whenever she told her lord and master can't come to impart some of his invaluable advice!"

"Don't fear, don't cry, my *little woman*," guaranteed Europe's new *man of the moment*. "No need to even once trouble your tender, impressionable small head. Your hero promises that our private Thursday evening get-togethers will continue just as before. He promises."

"That's ever so splendid to hear, Your Grace! As marvelous as this recent change in our nation's leadership is, this *little woman* doesn't want it separating her from the rightly world famous Alexander Markovsky!"

"Rest assured, my *little woman*, you will always be mine."

"And I forever *yours.*"

"It's a gentleman's obligation to be of assistance to his lady."

"And his faithful lady knows there's never been a better or truer 'gentleman' than Your Grace!"

"I'm deeply honored to receive such admiration from you, my special honey."

"So when we meet alone each week, Prince Markovsky will yet permit his *little woman* to blabber all her witless feminine nonsense?" pressed Celine, voice, meek, breathless, imploring. "So when His Grace condescends to visit me each week, he'll still permit me to nearly talk his ears off with all my nonstop, brainless jabber? His Grace, will still freely put up with me prattling on and on about subjects he's far too kind to ever explain are hopelessly over a woman's head?"

"Ah, but of course, darling," answered Prince Markovsky. "Prattle to your heart's content! In fact, the steadily higher I ascend in politics, the yet more skillful I become at diplomacy, the more too it seems I just can't do without listening to your silly jabber!"

III

The consequences of the *general election*, ensuing cabinet reshuffle, collapse of opposition unity, and the expected result of the coming presidential contest, all delivered effective control of France and much of Europe into the dainty, painted fingers of Marie-Therese-Celine de Montfort.

"I absolutely oppose women participating in politics!" she reiterated to her swarming, obedient press. "A woman's intended role is that of *mother, nurturer, faithful helpmate*. Her calling is to raise a loving Christian family and set for them each a good personal example. Women were never meant to enter the loud, cutthroat, dog-eat-dog public arena."

The countess soon amended, "However, while politics is undoubtedly men's rightful preserve, women are still obligated providing their own mother's nurturer's faithful helpmate's soft encouragement."

Henceforth, no piece of legislation was enacted, no measure of foreign policy implemented, not a single important figure in the country's military command, diplomatic corps, or homeland civil service was either appointed, promoted, rewarded, or disciplined without the government first obtaining the subtle, indirect approval of the lady at No. 3 Rue Artemis.

Already a renown classical pianist, an aristocratic beauty seeming just stepped from a Gordon Parks photograph in *Vogue*, a celebrity with mobs of ardent fans, Madame de Montfort now too revealed herself to be a major player in European statecraft.

She was soon often depicted in opposition newspaper political cartoons—a reluctant, backhanded acknowledgment of the lady's skill at keeping all her enemies at impotent bay. In one cartoon, Celine appears as a statuesque, regal swan gliding gracefully across the water, a long line of scruffy baby swans (representing National Chamber of Deputies) paddling dutifully after. In a second cartoon, she returned to fetching human form and wearing her signature strapless gown, Celine merrily plays with a yo-yo (marked *France*). In a third drawing, Celine is sketched as a department store shopper, she offering a demure, eye-batting, "Who, little me?" coquettish smile to a flock of enraptured salesmen (marked *Government*). These supplicants falling over each other in a desperate scramble to give their customer all the company's best merchandise, free. A fourth illustration portrays Celine, sly smile on lovely face, seated at a Moulin Rouge vaudeville keyboard. She is instructing President Markovsky, dressed in drag, to obediently make a fool of himself dancing the *cancan*.

The implication of these and similar pictures? Answer: if she refusing formal entry, Celine unquestionably dominates French politics from without! Yet even the most hostile cartoon inevitably betrays that its artist harbors a degree of secret admiration for this uniquely distinguished lady.

Mama's fame inevitably drew public attention to her children. France's widest read, most popular scandal sheet gushed in the purplest of purple prose:

> *If possibly not destined for the Olympian heights of Celine the Great, her two daughters will also definitely leave lasting marks on exclusive, smart, society. This particular article in our in-depth series concerns Madame de Montfort's younger offspring, the charming, seductive Rolande. Already more*

than a few gentlemen of wide fame and influence are said to be finding their craniums turned irresistibly and permanently in that girl's lovely, titillating direction! More than a few grand dames long convinced themselves to be each the paradigm of refined femininity are now consumed with raging, helpless envy, vain, impotent jealousy at the faintest sight of the charming newcomer's magnificent bare shoulders, excellent bust and stunning legs. That red hair?—It's real not dyed! Her queenly deportment, her gracious personal demeanor, ability to capture all eyes when making a dramatic entrance easily cause observers forget 1789 ever happened! What did Talleyrand say? "People not born before the Revolution will ever understand how sweet life can be." Perhaps, Mademoiselle Rolande can still give us a peek anyway? Ladies will be kept well-abreast of all further exciting developments.

So the same rag ejaculated to its millions of loyal readers in following overwrought issue:

What's Rolande's trick? She sticks to the basics! Ultimately, it all comes down to the basics. In this excessively pigeon-holed, over-specialized world we find ourselves, we often become so concerned, so obsessed with minor, superfluous petty details we forget what's really important. Not so, Rolande. And, therein is the cause for her remarkable and so speedy rise to prominence in elite, exclusive, smart circles. She knows to cross her legs, understands how a lady should exit a car. She's extremely good-looking, attractive also in that clear, fresh, uncomplicated, unquestionably innocent way. That's a form of feminine loveliness so increasingly rare in these circus clown's-worth of glop on face, dark roots, push-up bra, don't-trust-what-you-see, Americanized-days. Rolande's, is a pure, honest, unqualified beauty. A kind, so precious to keep hold-of on the increasingly few blessed episodes it now makes appearance. With instinctive good manners and superb taste in fashion, the girl speaks in a soft, fetching, melodic voice uniquely her own. She doesn't ask prying questions, understands exactly when to shift the conversation, what topics to avoid. If nearly all women are born-chatterboxes, gentlemen know this particular one is trusted with a secret. No feminist she, the young lady defers at all times "to her gentleman's infinitely superior judgment"—or at least like her Mama, carefully makes sure gentleman thinks so! She has far more clever brains and penetrating thoughts in her little head than those gentlemen—if they really are gentlemen— possess in their weighty skulls to even once fathom! So that's it, that's her trick! Simple but like E=MC2 most great truths are simple. Minor details just get in the way! Is Rolande ever her Mama's baby! As promised earlier, you'll be kept fully abreast of all further exciting developments.

"You better ask the lady first." The ship of state sailed proudly on, a gentle but firm hand steadily at the wheel.

Brigadier Aslan

FURTHER TIME ELAPSED.

Seasons passing.

So too unveiling human events.

A familiar long, sleek, shiny, feline black stretch limousine arrived outside the front entrance of No. 3 Rue Artemis. Last seen here transporting a young lady home from her previous visit to Neuilly, this exclusive vehicle reappeared to fetch her back. As all *smart* society and scandal sheet readers knew, Rolande de Montfort, like the impressive vehicle she rode, belonged to a prince, one, now also the president of France.

"Good morning, Brigadier Aslan!" greeted Mama from atop white marble steps.

"Good morning, Madame Celine!" replied the Turkish chauffeur emerging from the limousine driver's seat. He was dressed in jodhpurs livery, cavalry boots. A fifty hollow-nose bullet-clip semiautomatic was at belt. His late-forties, mustached-face was handsome in a rough, independent, non-gingerbreadman, non-pretty-boy fashion. If he almost old enough to be his longtime-friend's father, the powerful arms and hands of the Turkish chauffeur's athletic, six-foot-six-inches body could still untwist horseshoes. And then, if Celine requested, as she usually did since first watching the spectacle performed at her fifth birthday party, immediately re-twist the horseshoes into former shape.

That original spring afternoon in the atrium of No. 3 Rue Artemis, when he substituting at the party for a clown otherwise engaged, remained as vivid, dear, and priceless in the strongman's mind as if it occurring just yesterday. No sooner did he begin speaking this current morning, than the fond recollection from years past re-embraced his consciousness as an immediate, living, and tangibly beautiful experience.

*****

"Awesome! That's so, so awesome! You've really got muscles, Brigadier Aslan! Can you, perhaps, do that trick in reverse too?"

"Oh, but course, chere petite, just watch!"

"Ooh! Ooh! That's even more than awesome! You're really powerful, Brigadier Aslan! When did you first learn to do that?"

"When I was...Private Aslan."

"You were a private once, Brigadier Aslan?"

"Yes, I was once a private, chere petite! I was a private once. As with these horseshoes, there's hardly anything at all a person can't do, can't rise to achieve, if that same person simply puts his mind to it, put's his faith, his trust in something greater than himself. Little girls can do it too! And don't you forget that, ma cherie! And don't you ever forget that! Not however that I'll ever permit my sweet, unparalleled, miniature princess to become just a brawny muscleman like me! There are far nobler, grander skills intended for my princess's small, soft hands, far nobler, grander thoughts and ambitions are meant to occupy her talented, gentle, delicate mind than those a lowly soldier like me could ever even only once dare hope accomplish!"

"If you say so, Brigadier Aslan."

"Yes, I do, chere petite! Remember, don't contradict your elders."

"I promise, Brigadier Aslan."

"That's the brigadier's little girl! Now no more serious, tiresome, grown-up talk for the moment. You and I will have more than enough time for that together in years to come, you and me. Now watch, chere petite! Watch me with the horseshoes a second time!"

"Ooh! Ooh! Awesome! Awesome! Brigadier Aslan, you're like someone in the movies! You're like in those stories about Hercules, Brigadier Aslan! But no, you're not in the movies, you're real! And you're not in stories either! You really are Hercules! My own Hercules! I hope I didn't make you tired, though, Brigadier Aslan? I know I'm the birthday girl but still! Please don't tell me I wore you out, Brigadier Aslan?"

"No need for you to be upset, chere petite! Still bless you for asking. You're always so pious, considerate, kind, well-behaved, and dainty. I once believed a child like you was found only in movies or in stories! But no, ma cherie, you're also real flesh and blood! If I'm your 'own Hercules,' you're my own precious darling! I want nothing more in life than to make you happy, content, rightly satisfied for me to keep you as a shining example for the whole world to honor and follow! It's also exactly what you so deserve! Both to have and to be, my divine child. Making you always happy, forever a shining example is precisely what should be your 'own Hercules's' solemn responsibility, his sole desire and purpose in life! Straighten your socks!"

"Oh, I'm sorry Brigadier Aslan. I won't be untidy."

"Ah! That's much better! A good little girl straightens her socks."

"Still, isn't there anything, anything…any favor, help…I can do for you, Brigadier Aslan if we're going to be such special, lifelong friends? You said I must never forget to be a pious, kind, well-behaved young lady who keeps her socks straight. You told me I must never forget to honor my elders. For as long as I can think, of you've been my favorite elder, the elder who cares for me and is interested in me the most! What can I please do for you, Brigadier Aslan? Please, please, please!"

"Let me always love you?"

"On the condition I'm permitted to always love you in return, Brigadier Aslan."

*****

"I've come to collect, Mademoiselle Rolande," advised the chauffeur, no horseshoes brought along this morning. Taking out a long rag, he supplied additional touches of shine to the limousine's roof. "Mademoiselle Rolande understands President Markovsky expects her delivered to him each Friday at noon exactly. I assume she's ready?"

"Aren't you quite early this week, Brigadier Aslan?" questioned his former drooped-socks *birthday girl* now wearing pantyhose. She stood atop the white marble staircase descending from the *Baroque* townhouse's open oak-frame, glass-panel door. Then, after pensive, eager pause, she giggled. "Still, coming so early will give me more awesome time to see you and for us to talk!"

Click, click, click, click of woman's shoes resounding.

Madame de Montfort raced down the steps as fast as spiked heels allowed.

Reaching the bottom, immediately assuming jackknife-straight attention, she delivered her *"my own Hercules"* an ardent, loyal, *I-hope-I'm-performing-this-like-a-big-girl-now* salute. Clicking heels of imaginary flat Mary Janes, her fresh, moist, deep, so feminine green eyes cast longtime hero a five-year-old's trusting, deferential twinkle. "No, I mean it will give us *really* awesome time yo talk!"

As though she returned in mind, soul, if not flesh to an earlier, finer, simpler, more hopeful time, the endearing smile of a lonely warrior's *precious sweetheart* arose on adult-Madame de Montfort's all-too- knowledgeable lips. The heart of a tender, trusting brigadier's *little princess* made an additional exhilarated beat within the grand courtesan's now cynical, disabused chest. Soon, her virginal legs skipped merrily about the entranceway, playing imaginary hopscotch before later, settling in place to jump unseen rope. Long cherry blond hair completely covered the innocent power broker's face. At last, worn-out from all the terrific fun, *cherie* in pinafore, adjusted today's short pattern floral dress.

"Normally," remarked Madame de Montfort, still out-of-breath from jumping rope, "normally you come at ten o'clock, Brigadier Aslan. *Missy* and her mama are now still eating breakfast." She gave another *I-hope-you-think-I'm-now-a-big-girl* salute.

"I know, Madame Celine," explained the Turkish chauffeur, fifty bullet-clip semiautomatic at belt, returning salute. He signaled to his little aide-de-camp that she was at her best behavior, that her uniform was in order. He motioned that his *chere petite* could now stand at ease.

"Yes, I've indeed arrived rather earlier than usual, Madame Celine," elaborated her *own Hercules*. "Sister Claire, Sister Genevieve, Professor Eisenberg, Madame Castellane and Duchess Charpentier—"

"They're poor, so-gifted, young martyred *Little Marie's* original *Five Disciples.*"

"Yes, sweetheart," continued the driver, "they're the poor, so-gifted, martyred child's original *Five Disciples*. They and some other early adherents of Mademoiselle Kedari are staging a demonstration against President Markovsky's domestic legislation. The vast majority of last spring's opposition, as you know, is currently either too exhausted or too busy bickering among themselves to make an appearance. Of course, that's only to be expected of eleventh-hour resisters, party crashers. For all their visible eagerness, seeming enthusiasm, vocal loyalty to a movement which others founded, bandwagon hoppers never possess enough spiritual, moral, physical courage to remain committed after their first defeat."

"That's most perceptive, Brigadier Aslan," interjected Celine, noncommittal.

"On the other hand," reminded the old warrior, "the *Five Good Ladies* have been committed to the child and the message she taught from long before Mademoiselle Kedari became *Mademoiselle Kedari*, from long before Little Marie became *Little Marie*. Sister Claire, Sister Genevieve, Madame Castellane, Duchess Charpentier, and Professor Eisenberg each accompanied the child on her *Hegira*, if you will. So these five, bravely keep the dear's cause alive. Nuns like Sister Claire and Sister Genevieve are supposed to obey, to be chaste, devoted. It's only natural they feel a *calling*. Secular but no less pious Madame Castellane was once a world-famous prima ballerina, Duchess Charpentier, raised in a convent, is also a five-gold-medal Olympic long-distance runner. So they too are accustomed to faith, pain, exertion, and discipline. Professor Eisenberg may be an agnostic, but she's still no less committed to Mademoiselle Kedari's memory through her own special agnostic's *vocation.*"

Added the soldier, "I can't say for sure how many other hearty souls the *Five Good Ladies* can summon into the street at this date. Still, no doubt they'll succeed in rallying enough true believers and be countered by enough police to keep the traffic along the normal route to President Markovsky's estate obstructed for hours."

"I sense, Brigadier Aslan," observed Celine, mischievous, "that you harbor more than a little admiration for the two nuns, the dancer, the professor, the duchess."

"Yes, it's true, *Cherie*," acknowledged the muscleman. "I won't deny it!"

"I sense too, Brigadier Aslan, that if circumstances were different, you would be one of Mademoiselle Kedari's original followers as well! I detect it more than likely that you too would've accompanied her on the *Hegira*, if you will!"

"Better you not let President Markovsky hear you asked me that, *cherie*!" was the chauffeur's amused reply in indirect affirmative.

The two longtime chums, big and small, erupted into furious giggles.

In time, Celine began executing perfect, graceful ballerina twirls.

These were same perfect, graceful ballerina twirls as *Missy* performed that morning on the embankment.

Like her daughter, Celine revolved merrily again and again and again and again.

Until, as *Missy*, dizziness at last forced her to settle back on feet.

Mama's cherry-blond hair covered her pretty face.

"So I'm taking Mademoiselle Rolande by a different route this morning," the Turkish chauffeur explained, applying a final stroke with rag to shine limousine roof.

"Well, accepting difficult assignments is nothing singular for you of course, Brigadier Aslan!" said knee socks *chere petite* now in pantyhose. She bent over with her hands resting on bare knees so she might recover her breath, give time for dizziness to abate. "I think you even enjoy the missions! The more difficult they were the better, Brigadier Aslan. I remember any time a mission was really dangerous, really scary, the odds of success ever so intimidatingly wide, the high command could always depend upon you to immediately volunteer! Volunteer and succeed! Awesome! If you don't mind me saying so, Brigadier Aslan, I think the high command took blatant, terrible, shameless, disreputable sinful advantage of your awesome loyalty! You'd be *Field Marshal* Aslan now if it were up to me!"

"I'm so grateful for your 'awesome' confidence in me, Madame Celine," thanked her friend, protective. "However, I don't think I'll be able to let you play with my field marshal's baton any time soon! The high command decided Brigadier Aslan, his tricks and escapades are now out of fashion. How do the Americans describe it...I'm no longer *politically correct.* The French government concluded that any further connection with me is no longer popular with the voters."

He estimated, "Today, I'll bet less than one out of five in the officer corps even once ever heard my name. Fewer still, remember me in the! During ancient times, so the story goes, when a Roman hero was given a parade of triumph, someone stood next to him in his chariot, and whispered in his ear, '*Glory is fleeting.*'"

"Well, I certainly remember your name, Brigadier Aslan!" piped his miniature aide-de-camp, she faithful to the end. "Upstairs I've got some scrapbooks in which I've collected every last photo, newspaper story, magazine article, or press release about you! Every single one! *Glory is fleeting,* so they say, whoever those mysterious, all-powerful...*they*... are. But not in Mademoiselle Celine's opinion, Brigadier Aslan! I never once doubted for an instant that a brave warrior like you, Brigadier Aslan, could and *would* and always...*did*...make it through the fray!"

She eagerly added, "And you deserve to be a field marshal! You deserve to be remembered! Celebrated! Teachers ought to tell children about you in school! 'Listen, children, you should know about an awesome hero!' No one is as awesome and bold and as fearless and stupendous as you, Brigadier Aslan! You also deserve a statue! Much more than many of the mediocre scoundrels who do have statues! And one day there's going to be an awesome statue of you! I promise! If necessary, I'll pay for it myself! Maybe it'll be on top of an awesome column!"

"Bless you, *Cherie.*"

"I'm only mentioning what you deserve in recognition of all your exploits on behalf of France, Brigadier Aslan."

Dizziness finally abated, her lungs recovered at last, Celine now stood upright. She pushed hair from her pretty face, reapplied lipstick, and adjusted short-pattern dress. Sensing the old warrior obtained immense pleasure from watching his *little princess* groom herself, she took extra time. She also made sure the soldier believed she didn't perceive his fond, pensive gaze.

"Be assured, *cherie*," Brigadier Aslan finally remarked, "that as long as I'm still located above ground, I will always protect and defend you, hold you forever at my heart. I give my solemn pledge *cherie* as a decorated French officer."

"General!"

Celine, clicked her heels, delivered a salute at jackknife-attention. "My awesome Brigadier Aslan," she said wistful, "my heroic leader of men! My Brigadier Aslan who won the Grand Cross of the *Légion d'Honneur*, who was three times awarded the *Croix de Guerre*, who was three times wounded in action, who never broke under torture, who fought for this country on three continents, who three times volunteered to be parachuted behind enemy lines, three times was promoted on the field of battle! In this materialist, lowest common denominator, Americanized world, it's so tempting believing people with principles exist only in books, old movies or in opera. Not me, though, because since I was a little girl I've belonged to you, Brigadier Aslan!"

His little aide-de-camp again saluted at jackknife attention.

Her superior officer acknowledged junior's salute at jackknife attention.

Two pair of yearning eyes linked loving, understanding.

"I've absolutely no doubt that if I ever call for help, you'll come and rescue me, Brigadier Aslan. I've absolutely no doubt that you'll always come to me, come for me, come to take me away with you," replied Celine wistfully in choked voice, tears running her brown eyes and soft cheeks. "Make no mistake! If this were another time and another place, *chere petite* would immediately ask Brigadier Aslan to come and protect her, to shield her, look after her, lead her, keep her forever in his arms and to his lips. And that's precisely too how God should have arranged it to be! Arranged it for me, arranged for you, for us both! Unfortunately, we're not in another time and in another place."

Two pair of comrade's eyes linked yearning, understanding.

Birds sweetly chirped.

Chestnut trees gently swayed.

The glass atrium where the last-minute replacement for a clown won the undying love of a certain *birthday girl* was still easily visible just down the way.

"So the schedule needed to be adjusted this week," reiterated the Turkish chauffeur with fifty bullet-clip semiautomatic at belt. He, now affecting a businesslike, aloof voice, pretending the recent heartfelt exchange never occurred. "Mademoiselle Rolande can still be delivered to President Markovsky on time, but it's necessary to follow a different and much longer, less direct path. This requires setting out an hour earlier."

"I guess politicians don't eat breakfast," remarked Celine, pretending the words recently exchanged were never spoken.

"Yes, it seems they don't eat breakfast, Madame Celine."

"Would you enjoy coming inside the house for something to eat? Would you enjoy having a cup of coffee or hot chocolate before setting off, Brigadier Aslan?" entreated Celine. "You'll be ever so impressed with my collection of Claude Lorrain, Georges de la Tour, and Nicolas Poussin paintings; my Han and Tang Dynasty Chinese porcelain; my Safavid Dynasty Persian rugs. *Missy* says I could open a museum! Cardinal Blanchard and his learned chums at the National Academy tell me I've got the best private art collection in France! Journalists call me *the Greatest Hostess in Europe*. I don't want you questioning my reputation, or letting me simply rest on passed laurels! I'll be delighted at the opportunity for you to observe my meager skills."

She motioned for her hero to ascend the marble staircase. "Likely our world will be a much happier, far more contented, thoughtful, amiable, place if those wearing trousers eat breakfast and look at pretty objects before setting out on their political machinations. My mother, Countess Marie, used to often tell Philippine, Léonie and me that 'An angry stomach makes for an angry mind' and 'A dull environment makes a dull soul.'"

"Thank you so much for offering me a personal guided tour of your museum and to provide me your internationally celebrated ladylike hospitality, Madame Celine." The old warrior sighed, deeply apologetic. "However, as much as I'd be delighted accepting your invitation, I have a busy, hectic schedule today. I hope that won't offend you. I know ladies of your splendid quality are extremely worried they not be considered good homemakers. If my refusal today hurts your delicate feelings, please find it in your soft, womanly heart to forgive me. I promise on a different, less hectic, more appropriate occasion I'll be most eager and honored to be guided through your museum and to benefit from your far from only meager skills."

"No worry, Brigadier Aslan. You've far from hurt my *delicate* feelings! I will, however, hold you strictly to your pledge to let me provide you a guided tour of my art collection and to serve you breakfast on a different, less hectic, more appropriate occasion."

"On my honor as a decorated officer!" the old warrior answered in affirmative.

"So you've charted a new route to Neuilly?" resumed Celine. "So energetic you are, Brigadier Aslan! No less so you've shown yourself to be these years in civilian life! It must be a quality a decorated officer— *general*—never loses. It's simply part of his nature."

She motioned to a uniformed maid in her early twenties, just arrived.

"Frédérique, tell *Missy* the schedule's been altered today. Inform her that the limousine needed to arrive early."

"Yes, immediately, mistress!"

Frédérique raced off to relate the message.

Anxious feminine voices and patter were heard within the house.

"*Missy* will be here directly," Celine advised the Turkish chauffeur. "It's simply my younger daughter is so excited being privileged once more to be at the president's side. The very thought has positively left the poor little thing in a flutter. She'll be with you directly."

"Yes, Madame Celine."

The Turkish chauffeur checked his watch. Next, crossing his arms over powerful chest, he tapped his left boot on the circular gravel driveway originally laid out before 1789 to accommodate horse-drawn carriages.

"Eke! Eke! Here I am!" cried Rolande, appearing at last. Girl's large headgear and short dress, sheer pantyhose and high heels, *Coach* purse in left hand were all pure white. Long fiery red hair provided splendid contrast. She had applied her lovely teenage face just the proper touch of makeup and no more. Jewelry around her neck and on ears was as stunning as not overdone. "Eke! Eke! Sorry making you all wait, but I'm so *witless, scatterbrains!*"

Rolande stopped to give Celine a goodbye kiss before scurrying into the second row seat of the limousine.

"Have fun, *Missy,*" said Celine. "Don't forget to tell Mama all the exciting stories when you get back."

"I promise, Mama."

"And don't forget to keep your legs crossed!"

"I promise, Mama."

"And don't talk with your mouth full!"

"Yes, Mama."

"And don't put—"

"*My elbows on the table or point.*"

"That's my best genes and *DNA!*"

The vehicle set off.

"May the Virgin forever keep you, comfort you and guide you, Brigadier Erdal Aslan!" prayed aloud Celine, watching the limousine recede into distance until it was seen, heard no more.

"You're a lofty soul if there ever was, or is, or ever will be, one!" said Celine, voice choked. "I can easily imagine you, Brigadier Aslan, being at Troy, or at Thermopylae, or Masada, or with Jeanne d'Arc! I can easily imagine you storming the Bastille, or being with Garibaldi on the *March of the Thousand*! Or being the very first to join General de Gaulle's when all seemed lost in June 1940! I can easily imagine you in some other similar places as well, Brigadier Aslan! You're a lofty soul if there ever was, or is, or ever will be one! And a lofty soul if there ever was, or is, or ever will be one, shouldn't be just driving somebody else's car!"

Celine jumped to girlish jackknife attention, delivered a child's steadfast salute.

"The nation might betray you, Brigadier Aslan," she said. "But never will your loyal-unto-death *chere petite*!"

Frank Conversation

"SO IT SEEMS WE'RE going a different way this morning, Erdal!" piped Rolande, lighthearted, crossing her legs opposite, correcting the angle of her impressive headgear. She knew only vaguely about the anti-government street demonstrations today compelling Prince Markovsky's limousine traveling to Neuilly by a more roundabout, serpentine, less-direct route. "How nice though! I much enjoy being introduced to new sights and places. Mama always tells me that if I let myself become satisfied with seeing only a few sights and visiting only a few places, I'll become closed-minded and produce only a few narrow, unremarkable thoughts. 'Journeying to parts unknown,' says Mama, 'is essential for *Missy* to have a healthy, productive, worthwhile mind and soul. It's especially so, for ladies!'"

Contemplating the lovely, unfamiliar. picturesque vista racing by outside the tinted, bulletproof car window, Celine's younger daughter rested her chin on her left palm supported by left arm. "Judging from what I can see—"

Screech.

"Eek!" squealed Rolande. "Heavens to Betsy! Oh, mercy! Goodness gracious!"

The limousine stopped short in front of a two lane-wide repair barrier. One, lacking any adequate sign warning oncoming motorists that road work lay just ahead. Brigadier Aslan cursed violently in Turkish. Then, skillfully directing the huge vehicle around the unexpected obstruction, he again proceeded along the thoroughfare at earlier speedy, confident pace.

"How's a poor female ever to possibly survive in this cruel world!" lamented Rolande in artificially frivolous manner.

"First, by behaving far better than she knows full well she can at the present!" suddenly interjected Brigadier Aslan, once more speaking in French. His eyes remained fixed ahead; his hands capable of first untwisting and then twisting horseshoes back into previous shape, remained on the wheel.

"Pardon?" asked Rolande startled, readjusting her jostled clothes and fiery red hair.

"By she not behaving any longer in that witless, mindless *pretty girl* way!"

Save for he occasionally acknowledging her as Madame de Montfort's younger daughter and as his employer's latest toy, Brigadier Aslan's present remark was so unexpected, Rolande needed several moments to fully comprehend the words.

"Pardon, were you speaking to me, Erdal?"

"Yes, I did, cherie," replied Brigadier Aslan, voice grown fatherly, protective, his eyes still fixed ahead, powerful hands on wheel.

Cherie? This was the first time he did not address the girl aloofly as—Mademoiselle Rolande.

"I told you to stop behaving like a *Scatterbrains*. Maybe President Markovsky can't tell you're pretending, but I immediately saw through the act the very first time we met."

"You did, Erdal?"

"I'd not the slightest, problem. I used to be the primary field operative in French foreign intelligence. If you don't believe it, ask your mama."

"You're a *spook*?"

"Yes, cherie, I'm *a spook*. In fact, I used to be France's top *spook*!"

"You don't look like a *spook*."

"*Spooks* never do."

Brigadier Aslan made a left, then a right.

"You're a *spook*! Ooh!" declared Rolande, enchanted, crossing her pretty legs opposite. "That really sounds exciting! Just imagine! I know a real *spook*! Better than that, I know my country's top *spook*! How so ever, awesome, *really* awesome it must be being a *spook*! And also being our country's top *spook*!"

"Yes, there were indeed some extremely memorable, quite enjoyable, very stirring moments during my *spook* years, cherie!" fondly reminisced the nation's former chief intelligence operative. "The government sent to Isfahan, Smyrna, Tabriz, Sinkiang, Ulan Bator, Katmandu. It dispatched me to Karbala, Mashhad, Samarkand, Tashkent, Djibouti, Alma-Atta, Ashkhabad, Timbuktu, Kano, Bangui, Kashgar, Nouakchott, N'Djamena, Bishkek, Samara, Merv, the Khyber Pass, and Tierra del Fuego! Also to some other destinations where it's not safe for good little girls to venture! I wasn't given the Grand Cross of the *Légion d'Honneur*. I wasn't three times awarded the *Croix de Guerre*. I didn't rise from private to brigadier, I wasn't three times promoted on the field of battle, or three times resisted breaking under torture by merely shuffling paper!"

"Timbuktu, Ashkhabad, Samarkand! It sounds exciting! Romantic too! Have you also been where *Little Marie* was born?"

"Yes, dear, I've also been to where *Little Marie* was born."

"Wow! That sounds ever so thrilling!"

"No, no, *sweetheart*. My career wasn't as you image from Rudyard Kipling or from movies and television. Nor was it like *James Bond* or *Indiana Jones*. No submissive blondes in bikinis, I'm afraid. No carrying out investigations wearing a tuxedo. No ancient curses, Nazis, trapdoors, or secret passageways. My second-in-command didn't wear heels. No sipping martinis and playing roulette with skimpy-clad beauties in Monte Carlo, or escaping assassins in magical caves or on the *Orient Express*. Yes, the government gave me a car to drive, but it was a secondhand *Citroen* not a flashy *Jaguar*. Sorry to disappoint you, cherie, but most of what a *spook* does is far from what girls your age describe as *awesome*. As a matter of fact, most of it is definitely not-*awesome*. Quite time-consuming, dull, humdrum…it's far from the movies and television. No, being accompanied by Sean Connery, Harrison Ford, or Raquel Welch."

"Is that so?"

"As I said before, cherie, I saw through your pose immediately," reiterated Brigadier Aslan, his eyes still fixed ahead, powerful hands on the wheel. "No one can hide his or her real personality, his or her real desires and motivations from me for more than a minute! Your mama, Madame Celine, claims I could have been an excellent priest. She's likely correct."

"Is that so?"

"*Spook*, priest...priest, *spook*...the two callings are much closer than you'd imagine. Look, think about it! Poverty, obedience, if not necessarily, chastity. Accepting celibacy, honoring a sacred oath, being sent on a mission wherever you're told. You, seeking to *turn* members of the competing faith. People asking for our assistance, expect *spooks* to tell them *the Good News*. They find a sense of absolution in confiding to *spooks* all their dirty little secrets, petty moral lapses, and ethical failings. 'Tell me more, tell me more, my child. Supply me with further detail so I can better understand the motivation for your sin,' I instruct the penitents as if I were their religious confessor. 'I can best help you if I know all that you're up to.' And far more often than not, I'm gratefully given access to what I'm really after!"

The secret agent reminisced, "Like Lyndon, I've ferreted out all the sex preferences, marital infidelities, peculiar clothing habits, and exotic fetishes not only of my opponents, but of my colleagues! Like Lyndon, collecting this kind of thing comes in handy from time to time."

Mused his former chum, "Like Lyndon, I find employing this kind of material can prove quite useful for obtaining favorable decisions, for winning quick, eager compliance, for persuading even the most fierce critic or recalcitrant power broker to see the issue from my own perspective! You won't believe which internationally known *family-values* advocate one confessed that he'd immediately put a pistol in his mouth if not allowed at least once a week putting a certain section of a little boy's anatomy in his own gullet! I bet you'll never guess which anti-Muslim demagogue enjoys being whipped by a fundamentalist mullah wearing pantyhose!"

"Fascinating!" exclaimed Rolande, again crossing pretty legs opposite. "You certainly are an awesome *spook*!"

"Thank you, cherie," replied Brigadier Aslan. He continued, "Also like priests, spooks are effectively divided into postulants, novices, and full brothers. They've got the equivalent of priors, bishops, archbishops and cardinals. Martyrs too! Why, one of our numbers was even betrayed for thirty pieces of silver and died on a cross!"

"Heavens to Betsy!"

"You'll be quite surprised, cherie, how often *spooks* become priests and how often priests become *spooks*! One of us even became a great pope! Like a priest or a monk or a nun, I early in life recognized I possessed a *vocation*. I from my youngest years knew I had a *calling*. If not precisely entering a convent or a monastery, I too in my own way *gave up the world, took the veil*."

"Please, please go on, Erdal," begged Rolande. "This is fascinating!"

"In more recent years, however, my superiors began increasingly to ignore my advice," confided Brigadier Aslan. The more deliberate selection of the words and cadence of his sentences, indicated reflection on bitter personal experiences from the not distant past. "In more recent years, my superiors increasingly challenged the validity of the critical information I unearthed for them. More and more, neither the intelligence I regularly brought, nor my interpretation of that intelligence, was deemed trustworthy. I was slowly but steadily removed from final decision-making power."

"Really?"

"My superiors, individuals whose names you, Madame Celine, are quite familiar with, no longer wished hearing the truth. The truth isn't always pretty! Sometimes, the truth is gravely disappointing. It can bring terrible unhappiness, leave us angry, lonely, and frustrated. But that doesn't make it any less the truth! On growing occasions, the valuable strategic and tactical intelligence I provided; the expert, professional, experienced advice I gave my superiors, was promptly set aside. Why? It was because the truth contradicted my vote-pandering superiors' newest preferred dogma. It failed to conform with their own latest pet, rosy theory."

"'What is truth,' asked jesting Pilate and would not wait for an answer," interjected Rolande, quoting from **John.**

"Most fitting, love!" complimented Brigadier Aslan. "Pontius Pilate, Caligula, Nero, Genghis Khan, Henry VIII, Louis XIV, Robespierre, Mussolini, Hitler, Stalin, Franco, Nixon, Colonel Qaddafi, Putin, Donald Trump—things rarely change do, they?"

Following a pensive moment, he continued his personal story. "Then, after a certain period of time, the self-absorbed domestic politicians' and careerist office seekers' preference for delusion, their repeated rejection of my own expert advice based on many years of field experience led to its logical and inevitable consequence—disaster! As a matter of fact, a long series of foreign policy and military disasters! These were not merely embarrassing foreign policy and military setbacks. They were most humiliating and quite public national reverses! They were catastrophes which for more than a decade severely diminished our nation's prestige and influence in the world. Even today, we've still not completely recovered. And all this easily avoidable pain and suffering was brought on our nation as a direct consequence of the government's willful rejection of my own counsel! My superiors never admitted it, of course! They never admitted I'd been correct all along. And they are either blind, cowardly, incompetent, immoral or, most likely, all these put together!"

"And they shall turn away their ears from the truth," observed Rolande, now quoting **Timothy.** **"And shall be turned unto fables."**

"Then, when a scapegoat was needed so these 'statesmen' might save their own necks, their own careers, above all their own appeal to the voters," disclosed Brigadier Aslan, "the scapegoat they those was me! The shameless, feckless, self-seeking pimps, midnight cowboys, threw their ablest, most experienced, most talented, and most loyal operative to the wolves! *Get behind me, Satan.* Now the intelligence community pretends it's never heard of me. *I know thee not.* And if we continue our original religious analogy, cherie, I've been excommunicated. After all my years of winning fame and glory for others, others, whose successful careers, fine reputations and place in history rest entirely on my own work, they declare me *anathema.*"

He elaborated, shifting the car gears, "That's why instead of still being head of French foreign intelligence, I'm now your chauffeur! Today, after all my former prestige and influence, *I am but a voice crying in the wilderness*," now citing *Mark*.

"By the waters of Babylon we sat down and wept as we remembered Zion," replied pretty passenger. She added, *"How shall we sing the Lord's song in a strange land?"*

If they taken from *Psalm 137* and not referring to John the Baptist, the words she just cited, thought Rolande, weren't entirely out of the present context.

"I freely admit I'm by no stretch of the imagination a pillar of virtue," admitted Brigadier Aslan. "But I'm also not a betrayer either! I don't rat! I don't name names to congressional committees, write tell-all memoirs or spill my guts on Oprah! I don't turn on my faithful followers. I don't claim responsibility for victories not my own. Above all, I'm not a traitor!"

He confided, "If I wished, I could easily reveal what's been done to me. Like Lyndon, I made sure to preserve written evidence recording all my activities. I could easily reveal who's actually responsible for many terrible things, many shameful actions our country would much rather either forget or believe never occurred. If I wished, I could easily destroy the careers of all those who blithely destroyed my, own! I could forever destroy the reputations and historic evaluation of three presidents and three prime ministers! But I won't. I'll keep quiet. I won't sink to the same level of those who abandoned me! That decision ought to atone for a few of my many sins!"

"For though the Lord is high, He regards the lowly," recited Rolande from *Isaiah, "but the haughty, He knows from afar."*

"That's so very kind and sweet of you, child!" pledged Brigadier Aslan, touched.

"Know the truth and the truth will set you free," advised Rolande, quoting *John* as she stepped across the limousine chamber to pat Brigadier Aslan comradely on right shoulder.

"*Be not afraid,*" the soldier answered with words from *Luke*. He added from *Romans*, "*Be not overcome by evil but overcome evil with good.*"

"*Wherever two or three are gathered in my name,*" counseled Rolande from *Matthew*, "*so there am I.*" She much enjoyed this free and spontaneous theological exchange, Bible-quoting contest.

"*Observe all the things I have commanded you,*" parried Brigadier Aslan too from *Matthew*, "*And lo, I am with you even unto the end of the world.*"

"*Rise, shine, thy light has come and the glory of the Lord has risen upon thee,*" girl with fiery red locks recited from *Isaiah*. The words selected were anything but random.

"*Do justice, love mercy and walk humbly thy God,*" answered Brigadier Aslan with passage from *Micah*.

"*The wise shall inherit glory,*" assured Rolande with words in *Proverbs*, "*but shame is the promotion of fools.*"

For a second time she advanced across the limousine chamber to provide Brigadier Aslan a sympathetic and understanding pat on shoulder.

"Mama will be pleased with how we know the Bible," said her daughter, gleeful.

"Yes. But I'm unsure Madame Celine would approve of the manner in which we brought up the subject," suggested Brigadier Aslan.

"Oh, I don't know! I don't think the Bible is entirely inappropriate. Don't forget, Joshua sent Caleb as a *spook* into Jericho!"

"That's a point well taken, cherie! My *vocation* is one with an ancient and glorious tradition!"

Markovsky's walled estate in Neuilly became visible down the way.

"We must do this more often, Erdal," suggested Rolande. "We're not simply reciting from the Bible, of course, but also allowing me to hear more of your recollections of being a *spook*. I'm sure there are very few opportunities for you to bring up the subject." She added anxiously, "That's if it won't upset you, Erdal!"

Brigadier Aslan gestured not to worry. "Actually," he explained in paternal, shielding voice, "our interesting chat diverted me far from the subject I originally wished to discuss this morning."

"We've still a few minutes yet to arrive," promised Rolande, crossing her pretty legs opposite. "We've still got time."

The soldier paused reflective, then resumed, "I've long strategized as to how best correcting a certain aspect of your personal behavior. I much regret not carrying out my *campaign* earlier. Probably it was the *bridgehead* I established with your mama, Madame Celine, this morning that at last spurred me to *action, launched* my *operation.* I'm a soldier and use military phraseology far more commonly than biblical." He shifted the limousine to the left. "I'm not trying to offend you, cherie! Much the reverse! I was raised to believe an officer is by definition, also a gentleman. One of the primary responsibilities of a gentleman is being of assistance to the ladies. Therefore, it was quite poor conduct on my part not speaking on this matter before. You playing the *scatterbrains, witless wonder, nymph, submissive pet, butterfly,* or however else President Markovsky wishes to see you pose, might be very appealing to him. But not me! I find it most unbecoming. I find it most unbecoming of a child clearly possessed of many exceptional mental talents and fine spiritual gifts, a child who is so undoubtedly the offspring of an equally exceptional and gifted Mama. Your mama, Madame Celine, whom I've known and cherished as my own daughter, whom I've kept close to my own heart since long before Madame Celine was old enough to conceive, you! Since long before Madame Celine even knew where babies come from!"

"And to think that until this morning I thought you hated me, Erdal!" exclaimed Rolande, her mane of fiery red, hair fallen in cute face, pearls around sculpted neck askew. "I thought you hated me!"

"No! I never hated you!" assured Brigadier Aslan, his voice loving, shielding, protective. His eyes were still fixed ahead, his powerful hands on the wheel. "I've never hated you, ma cherie! As I said previously, you're only a child. And a child who, like her splendid Mama is possessed of exceptional mental talents and fine spiritual gifts. What I *do* hate is the manner in which you and Madame Celine conduct your present lives. I see you belittling yourselves in the minds and eyes of men who despite all their titles, power, and material privilege, are by far your inferiors. Remember Shakespeare warns us, '*All that glisters is not gold,*' and that life, more often than not, is just '*a tale told by an idiot full of sound and fury signifying nothing.*'" Aslan continued, quoting **Mark,** "Or, if we also return to the Bible, '***What profit it a man if he gaineth the whole world yet loseth his soul.***'"

"I've often been worrying about that very same issue, Erdal!" confessed Rolande, with a mixture of hope and frustration, again crossing her legs, opposite. "You see, Erdal, I have no formal education. True, I'm a first-edition book collector. True, I can speak seven foreign languages. True, I've read and correctly analyzed tons of history books and have learned to easily interpret oodles of literary and philosophical *stuff.* I've even written a drama and some essays about the Middle Ages that Cardinal Blanchard and his chums at the academy insist are all 'real first rate, insightful, and groundbreaking.' They like to call me " our pretty scholar." However, I've also no kind of professional training. Who in the general public would ever want to read, to watch, or to listen to anything I write or have to discuss?" She sighed. "I'm starting to wonder if it would have been much better for me if I'd never—"

"Hush! Don't talk that way, dear," swift admonished Brigadier Aslan, wise and protective. "Don't doubt yourself."

At last rallying from near-paralyzing uncertainty, her thoughts returned to the transcendent, existential summons on the embankment.

"Erdal," asked Rolande, "do you think I really, truly can succeed at something else? Please tell me, Erdal, please! I begged you. Please be truthful, honest with me! Do you really, truly, seriously think I can succeed at something else than just being a courtesan?"

"Don't be silly, my treasure! Would I ever speak to you if I thought otherwise?"

"What might this *something else* I can really, truly, seriously succeed at be?"

The limousine approached its destination.

"A gifted, inquisitive *Missy* like you," advised Brigadier Aslan, "requires no help from me as to find the answer!"

Into the Belly of the Beast

SNAP, SNAP, SNAP, SNAP, snap.

No longer did the impressive vehicle's arrival and departure from Neuilly go either unobserved or unremarked by the general public.

Snap, snap, snap, snap, snap.

The sleek, shiny, feline black stretch limousine boasting armor plate capable of repelling three direct hits from shoulder-fired rockets without leaving a dent, its chassis designed to flip over three times while its passengers suffered only shortness of breath, minor bruises, torn stockings now approached the front entrance of Markovsky's enclosed, wooded, suburban estate. As the land battleship neared, dozens of paparazzi waiting in the hedgerows just outside, promptly lunged forward as if a single predatory beast.

Snap, snap, snap, snap, snap.

Each freelance photographer—Brit, German, Italian, or Spaniard—hoped to earn a small fortune by selling an especially unflattering, sexually-suggestive image of Madame de Montfort to one of Europe's lowbrow, cutthroat-competition, mass-circulation Right-wing daily tabloids, weekly fan magazines, or scandal sheets.

Snap, snap, snap, snap, snap.

In today's dark-roots, gossipy, lowest-common-denominator, Americanized culture, a particularly titillating, racy image of Madame de Montfort might well garner the lucky cameraman as much as one hundred thousand *euros.*

Snap, snap, snap, snap, snap.

A similar picture, which also included "the uncrowned queen of France" getting her seductive way with the nation's elected president, might garner even two hundred thousand *euros.*

Snap, snap, snap, snap, snap.

As their scruffy, damp, disheveled physical appearance demonstrated, a good number of the paparazzi had been lurking outside the Neuilly compound for as long as forty-eight hours. They were each willing to undergo filth, hunger, rain, wind, and cold on the offhand chance the opportunity for taking the photo of a professional lifetime might arrive.

Snap, snap, snap, snap, snap.

Once developing a romantic crush on certain glamorous individuals, the public's desire to learn ever more about its newest heroes and heroines often degenerates into unhealthy, even violent, obsession.

Snap, snap, snap, snap, snap.

Celebrity, never to be confused with *fame,* carries drawbacks. These hazards afflict both individuals eager to capture such transitory distinction, and those discovering this problematic notoriety abrupt thrust upon them.

Snap, snap, snap, snap, snap.

If soon discovering that this morning the limousine contained only Madame de Montfort's younger daughter, the paparazzi didn't consider their two days spent in the damp, prickly hedgerows a total waste. On the current market, a tabloid-worthy shot of *pompadour*'s second "best genes and best *DNA*" could still bring ten thousand *euros*. If not a small fortune, it was still a prize no freelance photographer surviving off upfront cash payments with no royalties, could idly dismiss.

Snap, snap, snap, snap, snap.

"Be off with you uncircumcised scoundrels!" shouted Brigadier Aslan at the paparazzi. Exiting the driver's seat of the impressive vehicle, he made a threatening gesture toward his semiautomatic. "Don't harass the nice young lady! Make any attempt disturbing the nice young lady and, you rascals, will forever regret it!"

The scruffy clan retreated to a safe distance before resuming their furious barrage.

Snap, snap, snap, snap, snap.

"Out of here, you mangy, demented, pimp, syphilitic, child bugger!" yelled Brigadier Aslan. He delivered a furious blow with right cavalry boot to the rear end of the last photographer fleeing the old warrior's immediate grasp. "Be gone, I say, you recessive-genes, impotent, bastard, son of a whore!"

Kick.

Fly.

Crash.

The unlucky projectile, a Brit, hurtled several meters through the air like a football before crashing down along the gravel driveway. His complicated Japanese gadgets knocked to pieces, the film cartridges containing the valuable pictures he sought exposed to sunlight, were now useless. Instead of coming to their beleaguered comrade's assistance, however, the rest of the paparazzi were delighted that a rival for obtaining the fortune-making photo was fallen out of the competition. The other pests continued their photographic barrage even more relentlessly.

Snap, snap, snap, snap, snap. Yet still more furious snaps.

Brigadier Aslan opened the passenger door and offered his shielding, chivalric arm. Rolande took the arm graciously and stepped out just as Mama taught a lady exits a vehicle.

"Remember, cherie!" her knight protector assured. "I'll be waiting for you here to take you away from all this damned muddle."

Snap, snap, snap, snap, snap.

"Thank you so, so, so very much for our conversation before we arrived, Erdal" entreated fiery redhead Rolande, never before feeling so sweetly girlish, innocent, touched. Wishing to better explain herself, to go into far more detail about her deep onrush of gratitude, she found amidst the frantic, hectoring photographers the correct words, accurate sentences, impossible to command.

Snap, snap, snap, frantic camera snap.

"Don't worry, child," assured Brigadier Aslan to his charge knowingly. So expert at reading others minds, breaking secret codes, he understood Rolande's sentiments fully. "Fear not, cherie. I know precisely what you wish to tell me. I'm deeply honored to be of assistance. We can continue our chat later under less hectic circumstances. Now run along. I won't be far away."

Screech! Rumble! Rumble! Thud! Slam!

Muscular young footballer bodyguards and brawny house servants first closed, then securely locked the heavy wrought-iron black gate to the estate's twelve-foot-high, red-brick, wisteria-lined enclosure wall. Visible from three angles atop the thick, tall, heavy barrier were camouflaged *shoot-to-kill* army snipers. The marksmen trying so hard to be unobserved, they only made their threatening presence all the more apparent, intimidating.

If the Markovsky compound was geographically distant from central Paris, communication through Internet, fax, closed-circuit television, twitter, radio, helicopter, together with mounting fear of terrorism—made Neuilly a perfectly convenient place from which a president of the *V Republic* might govern.

Celine the Great's younger "best genes and DNA" breathed easier once the gates to the Markovsky compound were firmly slammed shut and the cameramen kept away, at least for the time being. If mobbed by photographers at the season premiere of the *Garnier Opéra*, soon too she appearing on national television presenting the trophy to the winner of the annual *Prix d'Arc de Triomphe* at Longchamps racecourse continued public attention, Rolande found steadily more annoying, intrusive, and, above all, predatory.

"How does Mama manage it all so well? Mama makes it all appear so easy! Well, that's because Mama is *Mama.* She has more talent for this kind of thing than anyone who ever lived! No wonder the press calls her *Pompadour*! No wonder those political cartoons show Mama as a queenly swan leading all the men in government behind as ever attentive, obedient chicks."

Still musing over her recent conversation in the limousine, Rolande, wearing a short canary yellow and white dress, passed through a full-body metal detector. Next, slipping back on her heels and chapeau, she retrieved her *Coach* purse after its inspection by an armed guard.

"I hate those photographers! The bastards, the goddamned sons of bitches, dickheads, cock suckers!" she muttered under breath before checking her unladylike language. "Goodness, gracious, heavens! I'm glad Mama didn't hear me just now! Mama said her wish to prevent me learning that kind of vile speech is one of the chief reasons she won't permit me to attend school." Rolande confessed, "Well, I learned 'that kind of vile language' even without being permitted to attend school!"

"Take all the press harassment, paparazzi stalking as a compliment!" advised the handsome, imposing new president of France, Prince Markovsky. "Take it as a compliment, *sweetheart*." Then presenting his left, he offered, "Come, take my arm."

"You idiot," muttered Rolande, under breath. "You don't know the first of it!"

Since rising to power, Markovsky had refused to allow a single weekend pass without enjoying the company of the Montforts' *brainless female chatter.* If she long knowing him to be a horse's ass, Rolande now found the prince's self-important behavior almost impossible to endure. The charming fool remained cement headed, unaware all his recent political success was completely the work of Mama.

"You full-of-himself baboon!" quietly snarled Celine's *treasure.* "You're too thickheaded to ever know the first! It's all Mama's doing! Mama is the real president! Mama is really the one making all the decisions!"

"Come along," commanded the General de Gaulle wannabe as he took his weekend holiday diversion by her right teenage hand, proprietary. "The day to get truly upset or really worried is when those scoundrels *no longer want* your photograph or *no longer* wish spreading gossip about you!"

"It must be true, Your Grace," answered Rolande, projecting a vapid grin.

She allowed herself to be lead across the gravel path set between the front entrance to a sprawling *ancient regime* palace and its well-manicured private park with large, evergreen boxwood hedges cut into the shape of zoo animals—elephants, lions, tigers, bears.

The massive turreted baronial dwelling France's new president enjoyed calling "my modest cottage," "my humble abode," appeared like an obscenely expensive, expertly catered celebratory cake, one covered with orange, vanilla, and cherry marzipan.

Nearby too was a symphony of luscious, vibrant colors.

"My, isn't it lovely, Your Grace!" exclaimed Rolande, motioning to the vegetation. "I so adore flowers!"

"Aha," replied her host, his mind elsewhere.

Brilliant, fresh, happy shades of red, white, and blue; lighthearted, glorious tones of yellow, purple, and green commanded one pair of feminine pondering adolescent gray-green eyes. It was almost as if nature, decided to personally intervened to cheer up Rolande's troubled thoughts. Tulips, lilacs, begonias, orchids, roses, petunias, hydrangeas, iris, crocus, snapdragons, cosmos, clematis and delphiniums were visible in profusion in the finely kept *continental* flowerbeds running both sides parallel to the grand, historic three-hundred-and-fifty-year-old wedding-cake residence once occupied by Louis XIV's mistresses, Madame de Montespan and Madame de Maintenon .

"I so, so adore flowers, Your Grace," observed Rolande. "And today there are so very many of them!"

Magnificent flowerbeds expanded outward from the palace's front sweeping white marble stairway to an artificial fish-stocked pond with high-spewing black steel fountain, and white marble group statue at its center. This particular sculpture depicted one of the eighteenth century's favorite socially acceptable erotic subjects, *The Rape of Persephone.*

Rolande immediately turned away in disgust.

"Damn! It's that hideous contraption again!"

"Still not learned to appreciate great art, *sweet thing*?" Markovsky laughed, condescending. "Don't you understand by now that this work is one of the finest examples of the *High Baroque*?"

Her gray-green still turned way in disgust, Rolande offered a dutiful nod.

No matter how often Markovsky declared it to be a masterpiece, and his young companion, no sculpture expert, readily conceded to the connoisseur's estimation, she nevertheless hated this piece. *Despised* or *detested* were closer to the mark. Rolande loathed that greedy, entitled, privileged, expression grafted on abductor Pluto's lustful middle-aged face. Worse still, she thought, was teenage Persephone's apparent total acceptance of the belief women exist only to satisfy male sexual desire.

"Intellectual not-too-soft porn," the youngest *Montfort Lady* labeled this Bernini-spinoff work. Locating the story one day in an encyclopedia she owned on Greek and Roman myths, Rolande discovered that the creator of this particular rendition, perhaps at request of whichever balding, potbellied, middle-aged gentleman originally commissioned the group sculpture, clearly altered the facts. In the true story, Persephone wasn't at all thrilled with the role she'd been assigned without asking. The teenager fought back strenuously and gave Pluto a black eye and some severe lumps on his dirty-minded head before she, at last, quite unwillingly, falling only just partially under the lustful god of the Underworld's control. These alterations to the real tale made the statue even more offensive. In time, however, the dainty young scholar trained herself upon entering the garden to look the other way.

"The *sweet thing* continues to disapprove of my taste in art, Eddie!" quipped Markovsky to his chum, the distinguished, refined, dapper, if-always-slightly-inebriated British ambassador, Sir Reginald Coatesworth-Barrington OM, QC, DSO, OBE.

The two aristocratic buddies laughed as Rolande diverted her vision from the offending marble effigy as she frowned in sign of unmitigated disapproval.

"You see what I must put up with, Eddie?" Markovsky laughed. "This girl's the last person on earth one would think being converted to that *women's equality* mumbo jumbo. But such is our enigmatic world! Such are the consequences learned of assuming high office."

"Yes, Alex, the strangest things do happen!" reiterated in mock lament Britain's learned, sophisticated, debonair, if seeming forever-tipsy ambassador. "However, I've full confidence you will soon overcome any difficulties ever arising. You've always done so in the past."

"You truly think so, Eddie? Unlike our gentle, so easygoing Madame de Montfort, her younger daughter has started developing *notions*."

"No fear, Alex," guaranteed the dapper Brit. "*Notions* are only the creature's latest momentary whimsy. It won't last long. She'll soon get it out of her little female system."

"You're right, Eddie," conceded Markovsky. "Despite all her *notions*, she never forgets who's ultimately the boss, who ultimately commands, and who must obey."

Rolande curtseyed deep and smiled meekly to both men before clutching one of her patron's arms, penitential, submissive, with both her own. "Yes, milord. Yes, milords."

"Watch out for your silly new chapeau, *sweet thing*!" reprimanded Markovsky. "This one is your biggest yet. I don't know how you ever manage keeping it on."

"Please, please forgive me, Your Grace, I mean, *Monsieur Le President*," begged Rolande. "Mama announced last week during her latest television interview that all fashionable European ladies just can't ever possibly survive without wearing her own newest chapeau. 'It's for any fashionable European lady,' declared Mama—and she is the unquestioned authority on lady's headgear—'an absolute *must*' to wear this particular chapeau!"

Rolande admitted, "Considering its size and price, Your Grace, I mean *Monsieur Le President*, I had my doubts if I could persuade you buying it for me. Of course, I should've never doubted your kindness to me and I am eternally grateful. You understand that when Mama decrees, I've no choice but to wear her newest and biggest chapeau, there's nothing else for a fashionable lady to do? That's especially so, for me, a loyal daughter!"

She promptly bit her painted lips, scowled. Remembering the conversation with Brigadier Aslan and then how quickly she forgot the soldier's wise suggestions made Rolande mortified. The shame consuming her was almost physically painful.

"Christ! I did it again! I'm just another *scatterbrained female*!" Rolande whispered to herself. "I swear, I swear from now on I'm not saying that kind of bullshit anymore! I won't even do it once! I'm three, four, five, ten times as smart as that full-of-himself bastard! Worst of all, he doesn't even know he is, the oaf! Where would Alex be now without Mama? Not the president, that's for sure! Likely, he'd now be in jail. And that aria the idiot keeps humming out of tune! It's from *Lackmé*, not *Norma*!" Then after pause, she grumbled, "I do so wish Randy Sandy would goddamned stop calling me *sweet thing*!"

"Don't worry, *sweet thing*," counseled Markovsky, oblivious to his partner's lament. "Being a *scatterbrain*s only makes you a more darling creature to possess!"

"As you wish, Your Grace, sorry, I mean *Monsieur Le President.*"

While still loyally clutching Markovsky's powerful arm, what Rolande saw next, made all thought of the prince instantly vanish from mind.

Just ahead, collected at a garden party under an expansive green tent, were a dozen so exquisitely attired *high maintenance* beauties aged twenty-five to thirty. Each wore a height of Parisian fashion short dress, heels, and wide chapeau. Their bodily movements were natural grace itself. They too might easily represent a Gordon Parks photograph in *Vogue* suddenly come to life.

These goddesses elegantly hovered around a long picnic table with white *Alencon* lace covering. Atop, spiked-punch, orangeade, hors d'oeuvres, fruit, little cakes, and other finger food were amply to be had on the finest Limoges porcelain dishes. White-gloved members of the household staff in eighteenth-century livery, discreetly navigated the genteel crowd. The costumed footmen bowed respectfully as they either offered further munchies on sterling silver trays with lace coverings, emblazoned *M* at the center in Gothic script, or refilled empty crystal, long, slender-necked glasses. Those served pretended as if the household staff was invisible. Judging from their obsequious behavior, the servants appeared to believe they should be considered invisible.

If the majestic ladies were engaged in neatly-choreographed *chitchat*, they pretended their vapid banter was of the most profound significance.

"Is that really true, Isabelle?"

"So it is, Beatrice!"

"What's to be expected befalling a lady next, Isabelle!"

"What indeed, Beatrice!"

"Hee-hee-hee."

Giggle, giggle.

"Keep away from those munchies, Marie. They're a disaster for your figure."

"Thanks, Celeste. You're always so kind and protective."

"And you of *me*."

Another pair, Marcelle de Clermont and Chantal de St. Germaine, were notorious within aristocratic circles as bitter professional rivals. Despite this morning's heartfelt pecks on painted lips, present comradely snickers and squeals, repeated mutual happy tears and loving caresses, the pair actually detested one another with a biblical passion.

Just under the two's current refined merriment, each one stood poised to seize the slightest justification to snatch at her foe's long, thick, expensively beauty-parlor blond hair.

Both women, stood nimbly prepared to employ the barest excuse for ripping at opponent's stylish, tailor-made, low-necked short dress. Each was ready to use the least pretext to kick mortal enemy in the sheerest pantyhose shins with own set of red, pointy, obscenely expensive Italian spiked heels.

Yet, for those unfamiliar with garden party prattle, Madame de Clermont and Madame de St. Germaine appeared the closest, most affectionate of dainty, *knows-how-a-lady-exits-a-car-properly*, former roommates in expensive Swiss finishing school chums.

"Oh, mi, Chantal, love."

"Yes, indeed, Marcelle, darling!"

Mere sight of the dozen beauties beneath the green tent instantly captured Rolande's rapt attention. As much as she found Prince Markovsky tiresome, lamented how he permitted the girl steadily less opportunity to devote to her beloved medieval *stuff*, nothing worried Celine's younger daughter more than the possibility she might one day be considered by the illustrious dozen as not looking *proper*.

Approaching her supreme judges, Rolande let go of Markovsky's arm to readjust her mighty headgear. "I must demonstrate I know how to wear this chapeau correctly," she whispered anxious. "I don't want them to think I'm ever less than *proper*!"

Those about to render authoritative judgment on the girl weren't just courtesans.

No, certainly not!

Like Mama, like sister Ferdinande de Godefroy, Auntie Philippine in Berlin and Auntie Léonie in London, like grandmother Countess Marie, Great-Auntie Bernarde, those beneath the green tent were *grand courtesans*.

Ingénue *Missy* felt the same mixture of glorious anticipation, intense happiness, dread, humility as one does upon entering the court of a great, historic, whimsical absolute monarch. Pretty face and lovely adolescent legs grew shy, unsure. Healthy deferential lungs under finely expanding teenage bust breathed heavy. Considering the small, enclosed, isolated but immensely privileged social clique the girl appeared possessing no choice but to spend entire life. It was no surprise she awestruck.

"I must demonstrate I know how to wear this chapeau correctly," she whispered anxiously. "I want the great ladies to think I'm *proper*."

As yet too young to vote or sign a business contract, still living at home as Mama's legal ward and financial responsibility, Rolande understood she was still far from attaining the celebrated rank of grand courtesan. It was important she not let gossip column-jabber go to her head. "I must not disappoint them. I must show them I too am *proper*. I must show them I too am always *proper*."

If she fearful of making a poor impression, it was because this aspiring novice was already granted a certain degree of intimacy with her *betters*. While today was the first time Rolande confronted all twelve queenly figures united, she had earlier, as Madame de Montfort's daughter and Ferdinande de Godefroy's half sister, met each of the celebrated dames individually, at least twice. Those previous encounters occurring either on a Sunday following Mass; over tea at No. 3 Rue Artemis; or, as both attended the same formal dinner, public groundbreaking, horse race, or opera performance. On those earlier occasions, the renowned ladies each warmly praised *Treasure*'s combination of physical loveliness and singular piercing intelligence. All expressed deep admiration for *sweetheart*'s natural grace, excellent manners, and fine deportment. *Missy* hoped she still retained that high estimate among the famous dozen.

"Please, please, let it be so!"

Missy long yearned to be selected as one of these lofty dames' protégée. Then, in time, after she demonstrated her own clear, fine skill at the historic calling, *Missy* might be chosen as that particular grand courtesan's successor.

"Please, Blessed Virgin, let this be the day!"

Any of the famous dozen beneath the green the tent could at once fulfill their supplicant's so desperate, heartfelt longing. Through offering the girl just a single encouraging smile, knowing wink, welcoming flutter of eyelashes, or beckoning motion of white-gloved hand in recognition, a dainty autocrat might at once capture and forever possess Rolande's total and joyful submission.

"Take me, take me, please!" Rolande asked in stammered whisper. "I'll do all you wish, Madame. I'll do all you ask of me and more still!"

Each, she closer acquainted with the members of her elite clientele than were their wives, families, political or business colleagues; each, she firmly established as the only individual lonely statesmen, unhappy kingmakers, or insecure plutocrats can ever love, cherish, trust, ask for honest advice; each, she observed how frequently *weak* women are in fact wise, brave, while *strong* men are idiots, cowards—none of the pretty dozen beneath the green tent ever regretted allowing these dapper gents to take official credit for her own successes.

If none could succeed at this subtle, convoluted game quite as well as Mama, every player was still materially, financially, and politically more than well rewarded. All were fiercely determined the current social system be preserved, even strengthened. Far from she being a slut, whore, sponger, as "those neurotic, self-pitying, overeducated, short-haired *feminists* in trousers" accuse a courtesan, retort her comrades, instead provides young women a fine example to follow in life. She, ably demonstrates how much their own sex can still accomplish in what will always remain, at least on the surface, a man's world.

As much as she wished immediately divulging her passionate affection to the dozen, Rolande conceded professional etiquette forbade it. There were strict rules, exact procedures, clear guidelines needing to be followed to the last letter and grammatical mark. So that it continues receiving all the respect, exercises all the influence it rightly deserves, members of Rolande's vocation long ago established a code of personal behavior, a spirit of team loyalty, a group hierarchy as vigorous as any.

Members must at all times speak, dress, and comport themselves as *ladies*. If seldom marrying, and then only as a strategic maneuver to fortify her position in society, each courtesan is from her twenty-fifth birthday (wed or not) addressed, referred to, as *Madame*. Failing to do so is an almost unpardonable breech of manners and moral behavior. Conversation between courtesans at large events and with gentlemen present is restricted to *chitchat*. When smaller settings or gentlemen distracted elsewhere allow opportunity for *girl talk*, only ladies of a certain rank and recognized proven skill are invited joining in. As for those intimate, confessional *one-on-one* encounters leading to deep personal friendships, it is beneath a grand courtesan's dignity being *obliged* inviting a newcomer to her residence, or being *obliged* taking a newcomer out to luncheon. Additionally, beginners should not send grand courtesans unsolicited invitations with any presumption the offer require immediate reply. Any novice judged by her fully initiated sisters to be cutting ahead in line, being unwilling to wait her turn, acting too big for her miniskirt, is promptly black-balled until she learns her *place*.

If Madame de Montfort is today Europe's, *our Celine*, she too began at the bottom of the totem pole. She too rose only after she first demonstrating unquestioned allegiance to her profession's code of behavior, displaying sufficient *team spirit*. Her younger daughter was naturally expected do the same.

Rolande smiled at her heroines timid, beseeching.

A silent, mutually contemplative moment passed.

Followed by a second...third.

Then, wonder of wonders, in unmistakable response, the dozen beneath green tent smiled back.

The expression on each lady's fetching face was clearly approving.

Each regal dame registered her complete understanding, full acceptance of the teenager's humble plea.

Twelve pair of charming, genteel eyes beckoned.

Come to me, dear!

Come to your, mistress!

Come and be your mistress's obedient little darling!

Rolande gasped.

She'd passed the test, won the goal faster, sooner, than girl ever dared imagine.

One day, she would like Mama be—a *grand courtesan.*

"No, no stop! Stop!" cried a still, small, inner voice, One growing ever more forthright, determined, since its possessor's summons on the embankment. "Don't do it! That's not your mission! That's not what you were meant for in life!"

Rolande halted, made to flee.

"Erdal, Erdal!" she called, frantically signaling to the chauffeur. "Get me, quick!"

With paternal delight registered on his face, seen on his body, Brigadier Aslan jumped into the limousine and came to collect his young charge.

"What's all this about?" queried Markovsky, startled as his just moments earlier loyal companion abruptly stepped away. "Where are you going, *sweet thing?*"

"Not with you, Sandy, my boy!" answered Rolande, leaping into the waiting limousine. Then, after entering, closing door behind, she added through open window, "By the way, that aria you keep humming forever out of tune, it's from *Lackmé*, not *Norma*!"

"Now get me out of this dreadful place, Erdal," pleaded Rolande to the fatherly chauffeur. "Take me far away, as far away as you can!"

"Instantly, mademoiselle," the former intelligence chief replied.

"Also, let's exit the *other* way!" insisted Rolande, motioning they avoid once more passing the Baroque, marble *Rape of Persephone*. "Let's get out of here, the *other* way. I so hate that ghastly statue!"

www.ingramcontent.com/pod-product-compliance
Lightning Source LLC
Chambersburg PA
CBHW050455110726
47899CB00003B/946